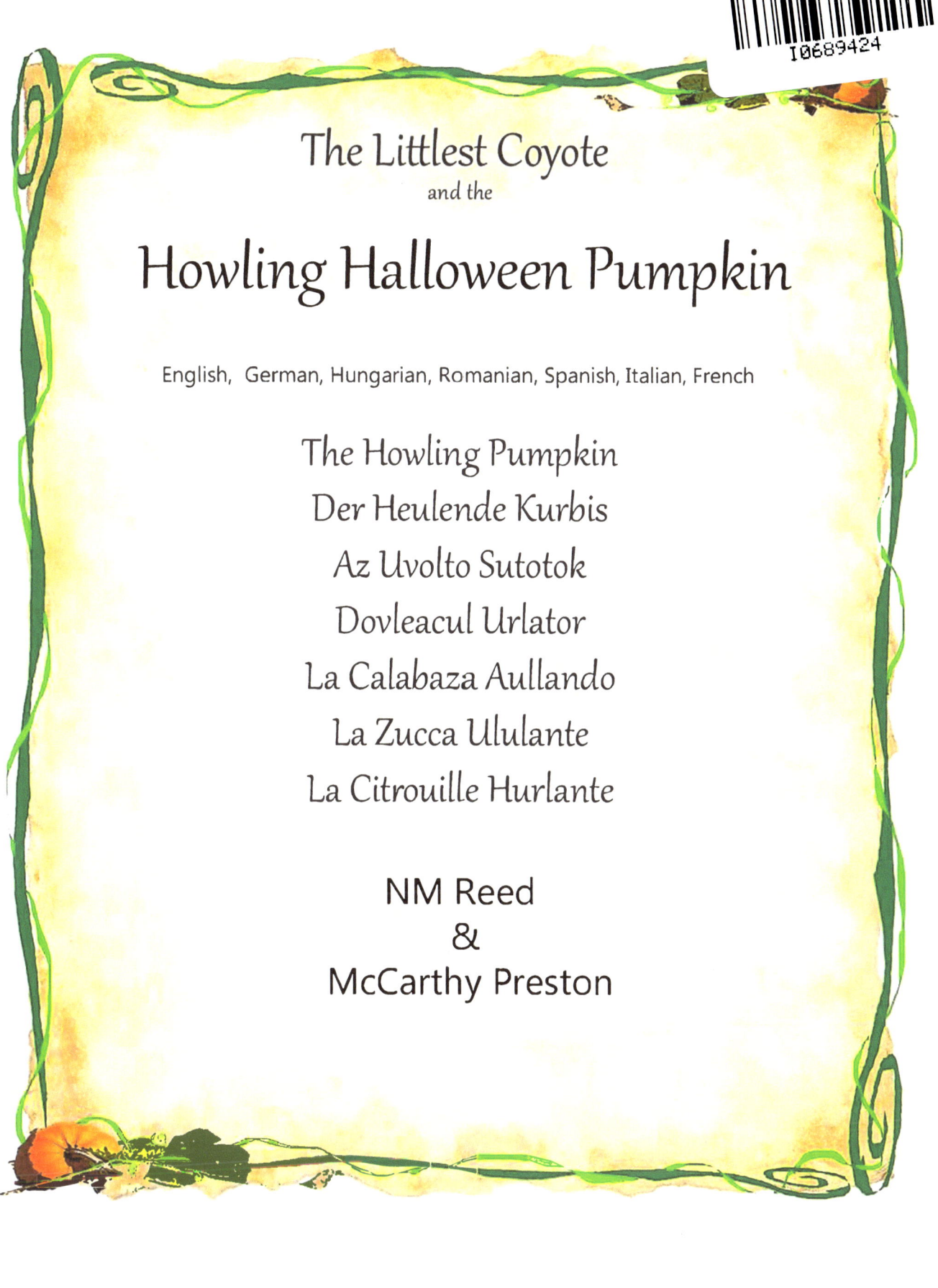

The Littlest Coyote
and the

Howling Halloween Pumpkin

English, German, Hungarian, Romanian, Spanish, Italian, French

The Howling Pumpkin
Der Heulende Kurbis
Az Uvolto Sutotok
Dovleacul Urlator
La Calabaza Aullando
La Zucca Ululante
La Citrouille Hurlante

NM Reed
&
McCarthy Preston

To order additional copy of this book, contact:
TatteredUntcornPublishing.com
NMReedBooks.com
StevensPressLLC.com

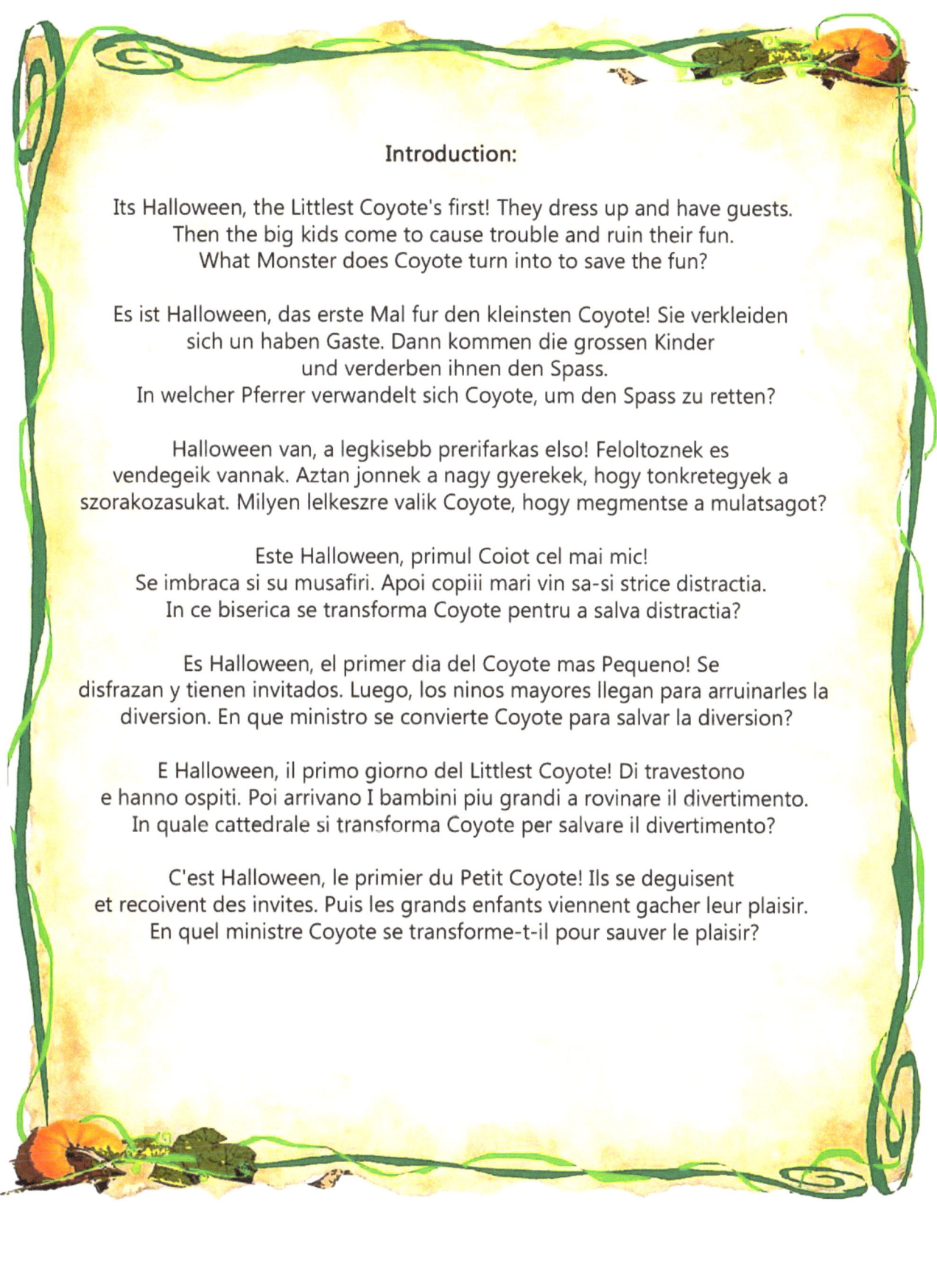

Introduction:

Its Halloween, the Littlest Coyote's first! They dress up and have guests.
Then the big kids come to cause trouble and ruin their fun.
What Monster does Coyote turn into to save the fun?

Es ist Halloween, das erste Mal fur den kleinsten Coyote! Sie verkleiden
sich un haben Gaste. Dann kommen die grossen Kinder
und verderben ihnen den Spass.
In welcher Pferrer verwandelt sich Coyote, um den Spass zu retten?

Halloween van, a legkisebb prerifarkas elso! Feloltoznek es
vendegeik vannak. Aztan jonnek a nagy gyerekek, hogy tonkretegyek a
szorakozasukat. Milyen lelkeszre valik Coyote, hogy megmentse a mulatsagot?

Este Halloween, primul Coiot cel mai mic!
Se imbraca si su musafiri. Apoi copiii mari vin sa-si strice distractia.
In ce biserica se transforma Coyote pentru a salva distractia?

Es Halloween, el primer dia del Coyote mas Pequeno! Se
disfrazan y tienen invitados. Luego, los ninos mayores llegan para arruinarles la
diversion. En que ministro se convierte Coyote para salvar la diversion?

E Halloween, il primo giorno del Littlest Coyote! Di travestono
e hanno ospiti. Poi arrivano I bambini piu grandi a rovinare il divertimento.
In quale cattedrale si transforma Coyote per salvare il divertimento?

C'est Halloween, le primier du Petit Coyote! Ils se deguisent
et recoivent des invites. Puis les grands enfants viennent gacher leur plaisir.
En quel ministre Coyote se transforme-t-il pour sauver le plaisir?

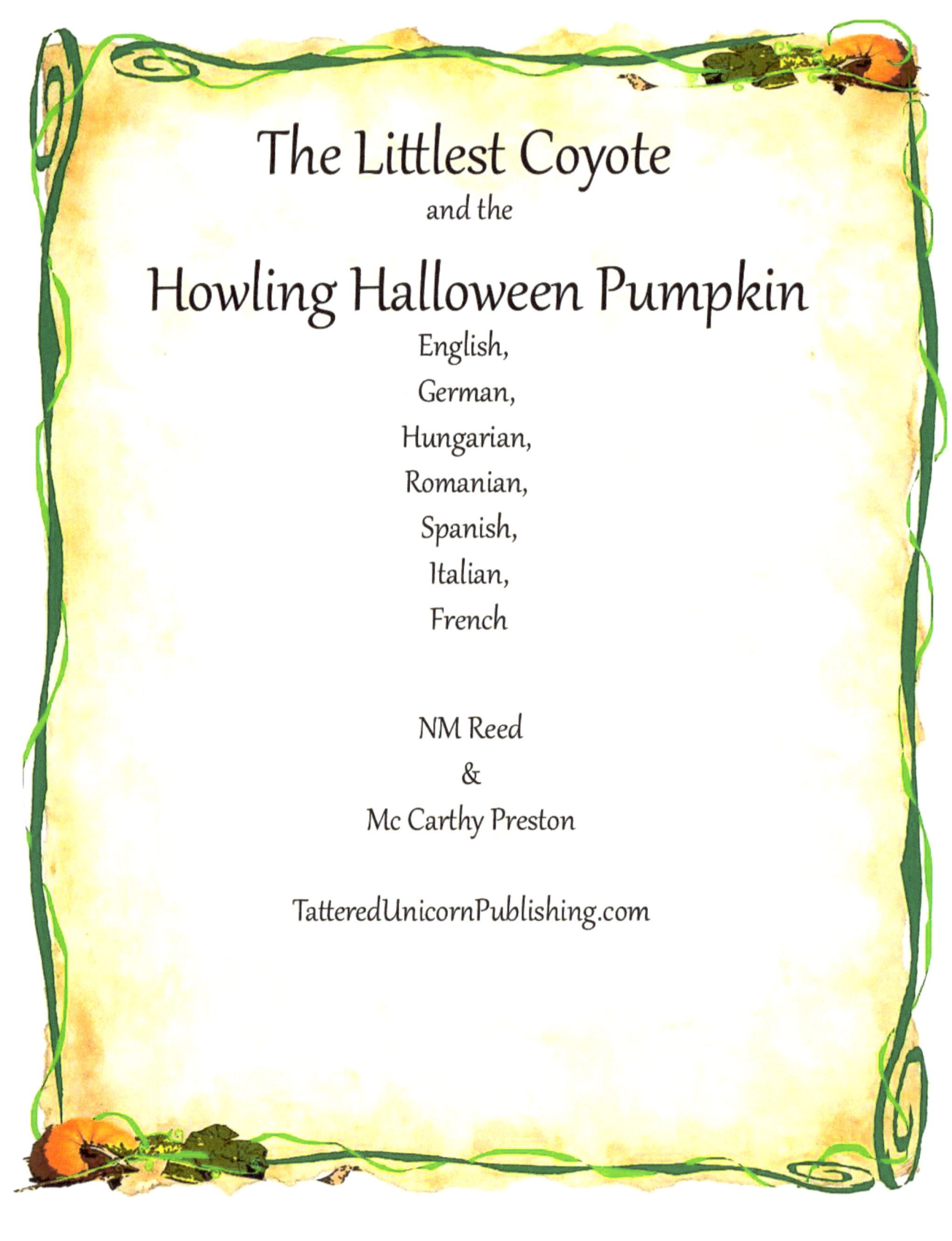

The Littlest Coyote
and the

Howling Halloween Pumpkin

English,
German,
Hungarian,
Romanian,
Spanish,
Italian,
French

NM Reed

&

Mc Carthy Preston

TatteredUnicornPublishing.com

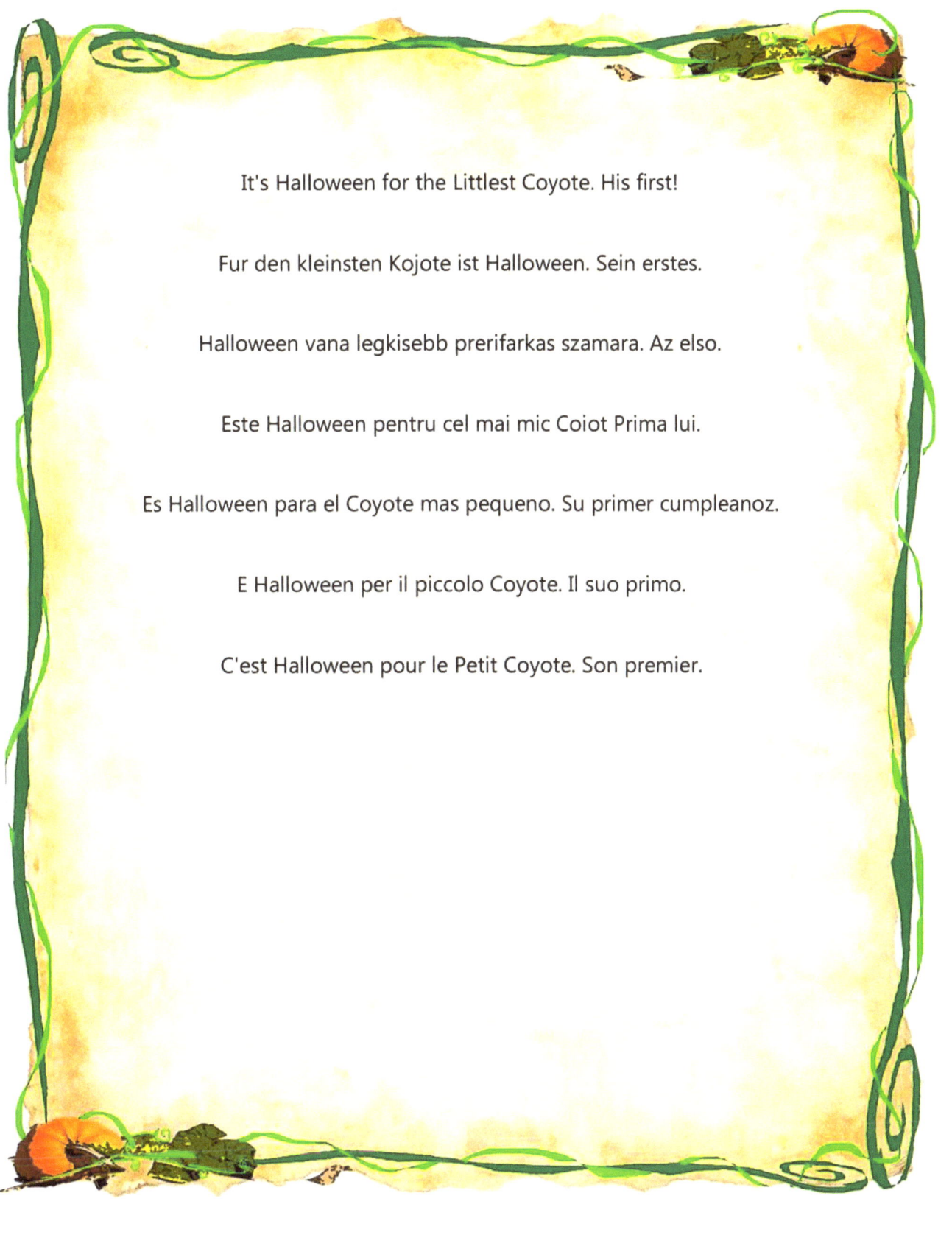

It's Halloween for the Littlest Coyote. His first!

Fur den kleinsten Kojote ist Halloween. Sein erstes.

Halloween vana legkisebb prerifarkas szamara. Az elso.

Este Halloween pentru cel mai mic Coiot Prima lui.

Es Halloween para el Coyote mas pequeno. Su primer cumpleanoz.

E Halloween per il piccolo Coyote. Il suo primo.

C'est Halloween pour le Petit Coyote. Son premier.

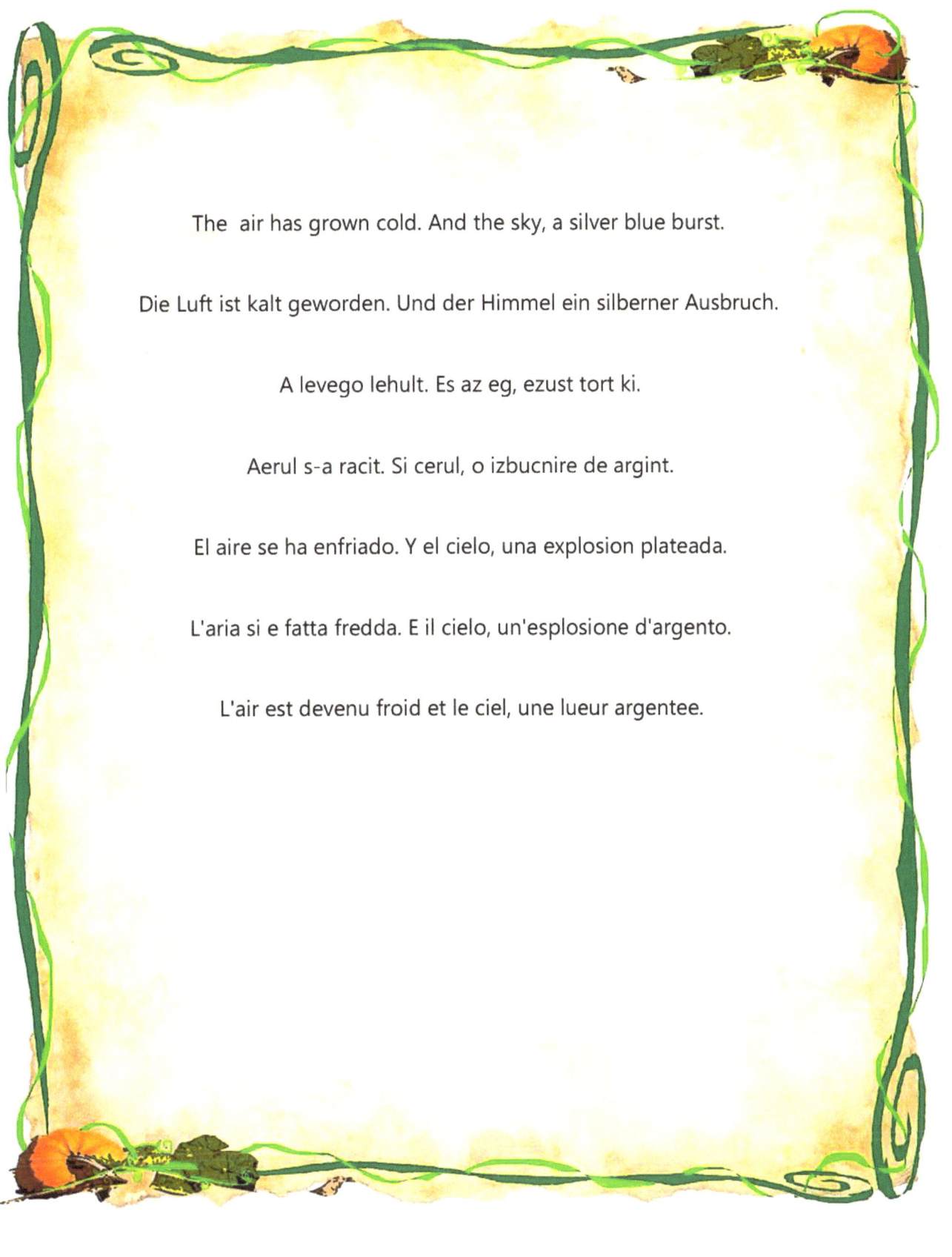

The air has grown cold. And the sky, a silver blue burst.

Die Luft ist kalt geworden. Und der Himmel ein silberner Ausbruch.

A levego lehult. Es az eg, ezust tort ki.

Aerul s-a racit. Si cerul, o izbucnire de argint.

El aire se ha enfriado. Y el cielo, una explosion plateada.

L'aria si e fatta fredda. E il cielo, un'esplosione d'argento.

L'air est devenu froid et le ciel, une lueur argentee.

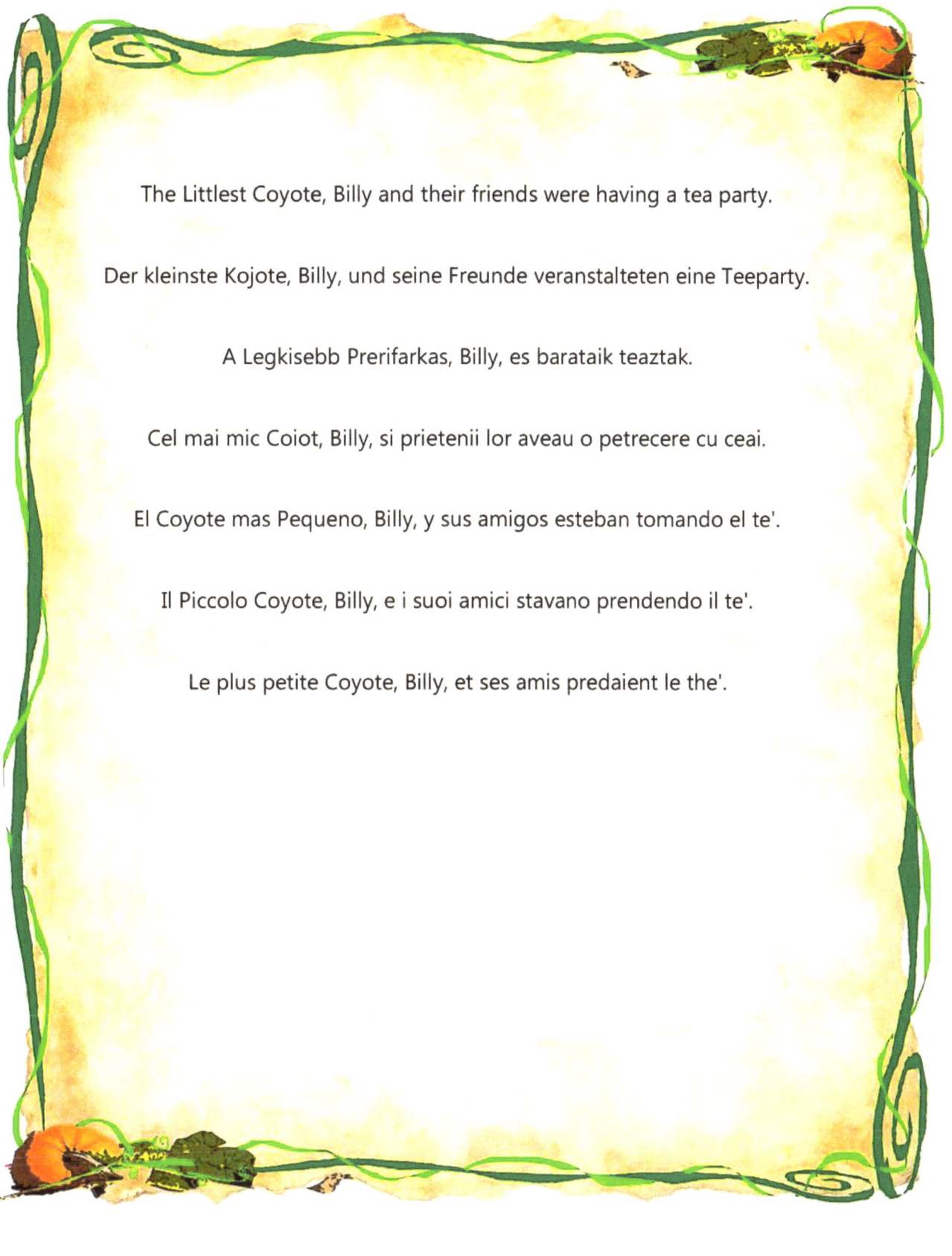

The Littlest Coyote, Billy and their friends were having a tea party.

Der kleinste Kojote, Billy, und seine Freunde veranstalteten eine Teeparty.

A Legkisebb Prerifarkas, Billy, es barataik teaztak.

Cel mai mic Coiot, Billy, si prietenii lor aveau o petrecere cu ceai.

El Coyote mas Pequeno, Billy, y sus amigos esteban tomando el te'.

Il Piccolo Coyote, Billy, e i suoi amici stavano prendendo il te'.

Le plus petite Coyote, Billy, et ses amis predaient le the'.

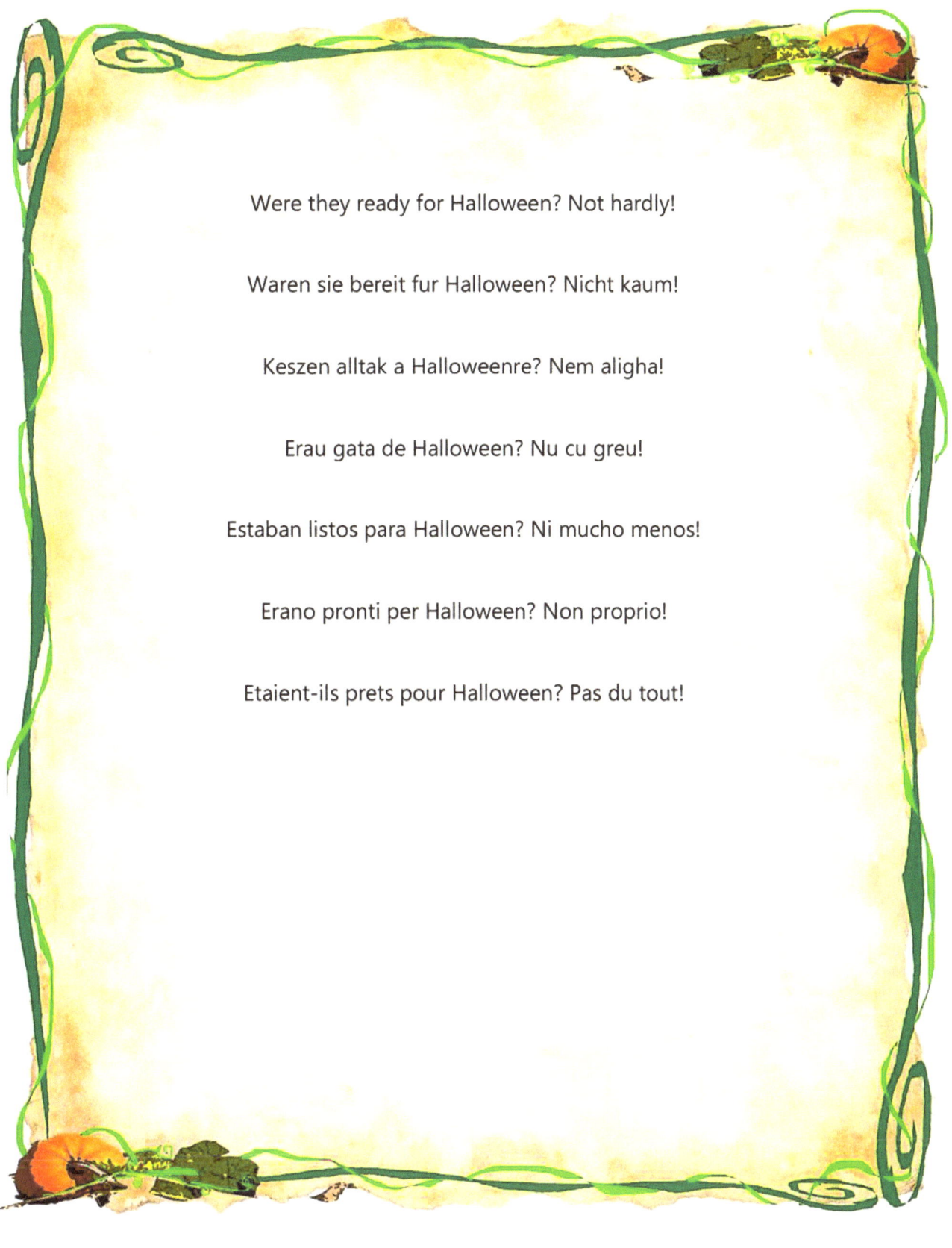

Were they ready for Halloween? Not hardly!

Waren sie bereit fur Halloween? Nicht kaum!

Keszen alltak a Halloweenre? Nem aligha!

Erau gata de Halloween? Nu cu greu!

Estaban listos para Halloween? Ni mucho menos!

Erano pronti per Halloween? Non proprio!

Etaient-ils prets pour Halloween? Pas du tout!

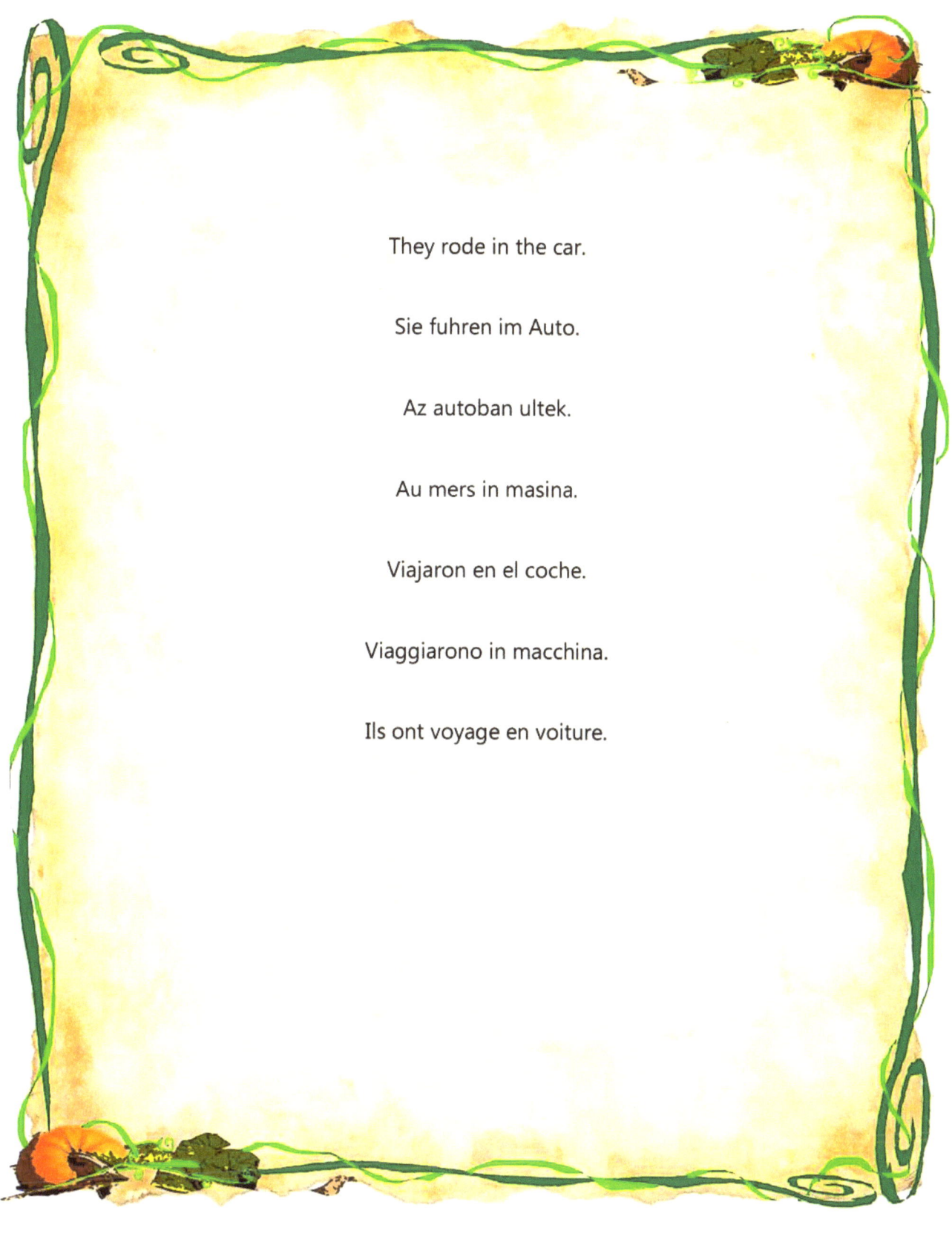

They rode in the car.

Sie fuhren im Auto.

Az autoban ultek.

Au mers in masina.

Viajaron en el coche.

Viaggiarono in macchina.

Ils ont voyage en voiture.

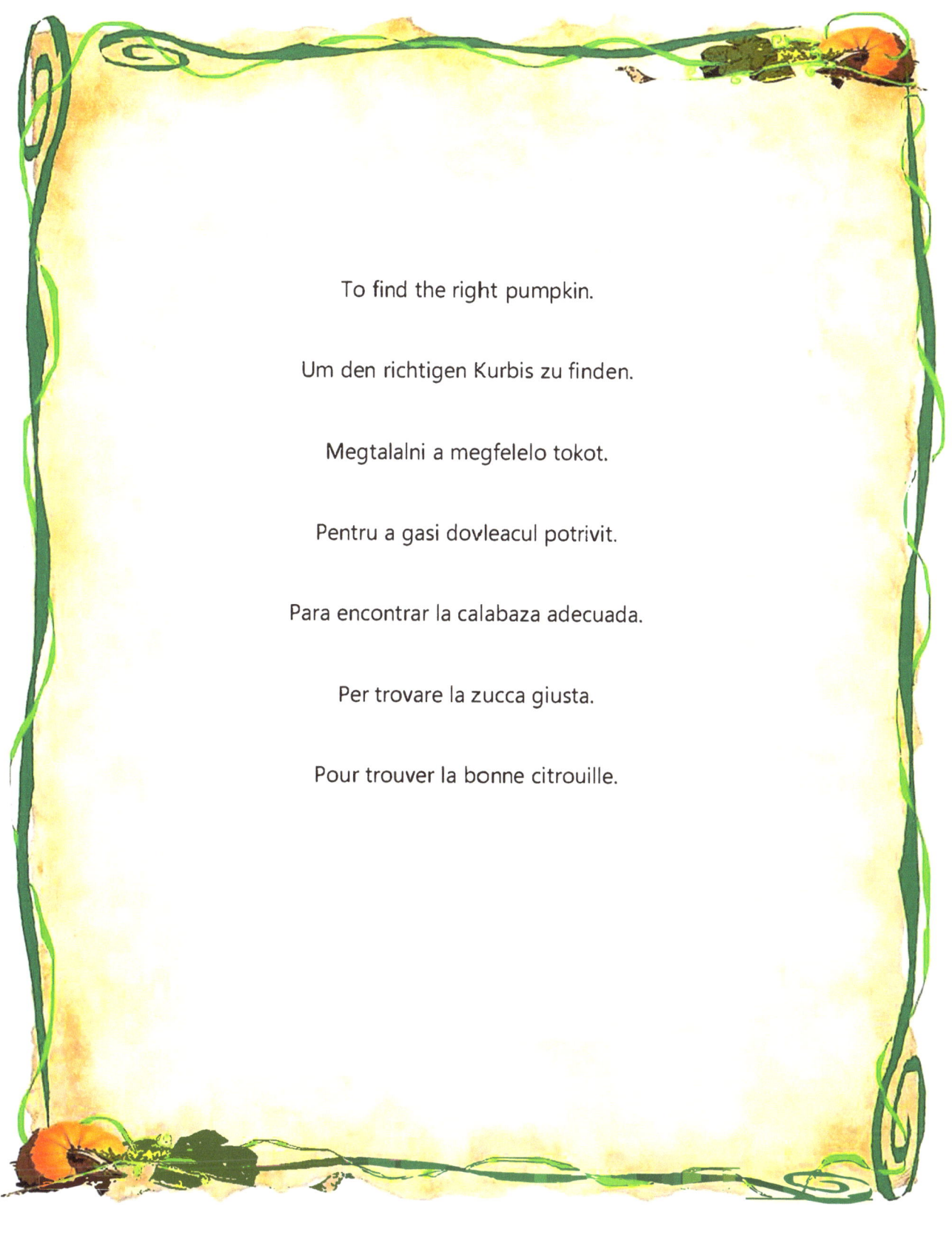

To find the right pumpkin.

Um den richtigen Kurbis zu finden.

Megtalalni a megfelelo tokot.

Pentru a gasi dovleacul potrivit.

Para encontrar la calabaza adecuada.

Per trovare la zucca giusta.

Pour trouver la bonne citrouille.

to find a huge pumpkin.

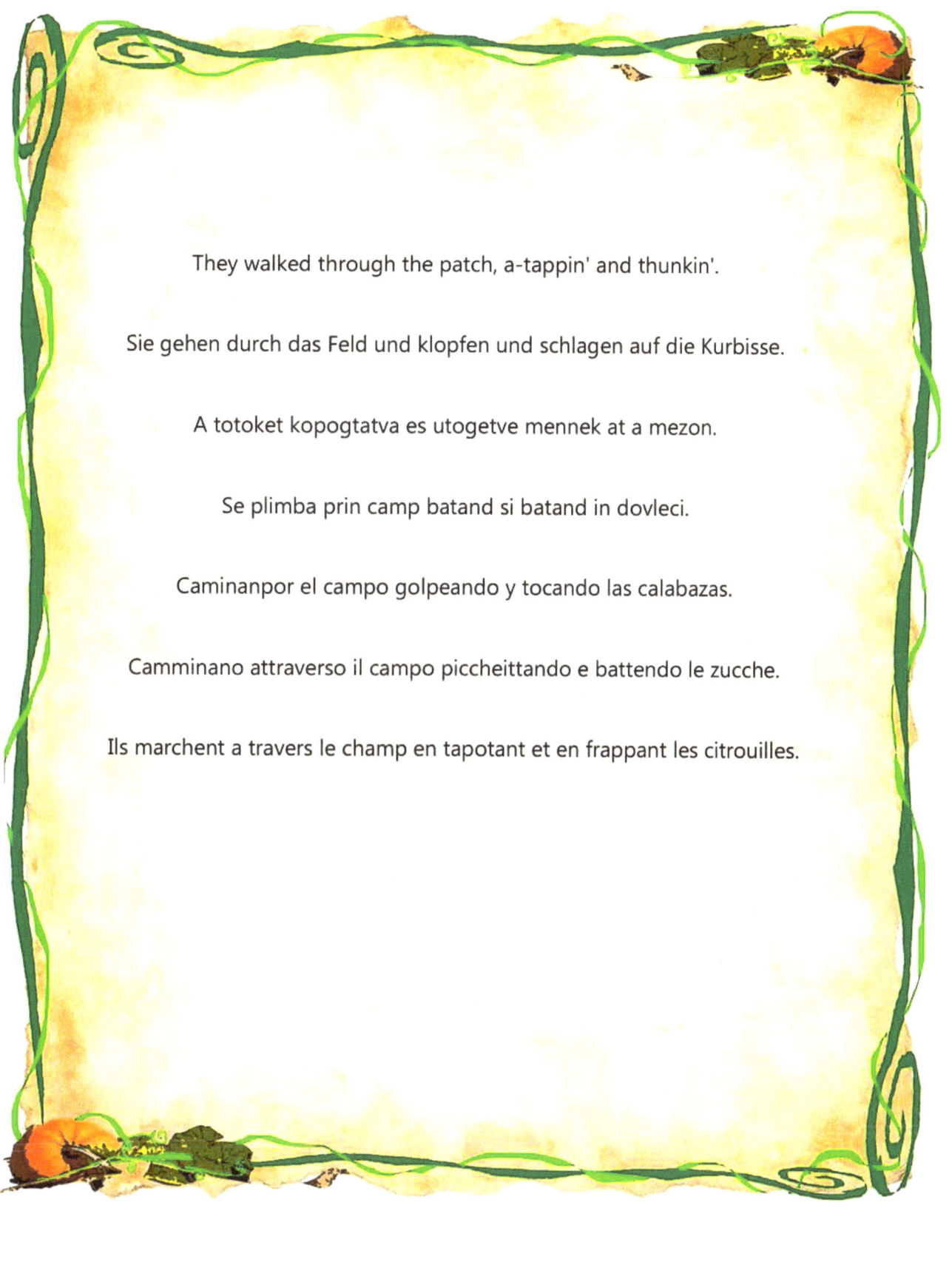

They walked through the patch, a-tappin' and thunkin'.

Sie gehen durch das Feld und klopfen und schlagen auf die Kurbisse.

A totoket kopogtatva es utogetve mennek at a mezon.

Se plimba prin camp batand si batand in dovleci.

Caminanpor el campo golpeando y tocando las calabazas.

Camminano attraverso il campo piccheittando e battendo le zucche.

Ils marchent a travers le champ en tapotant et en frappant les citrouilles.

They searched for a globe with just the right hue.

Sie suchten nach einem Globus mit genau dem richtigen Farbton.

Olyan foldgombot kerestek, amelynek megfelelo arnyalata van.

Au cautat un glob cu nuanta potrivita.

Buscaron un globo con el tono justo.

Hanno cercato un globo con la giusta tonalita.

Ils cherchaient un globe avec juste la bonne teinte.

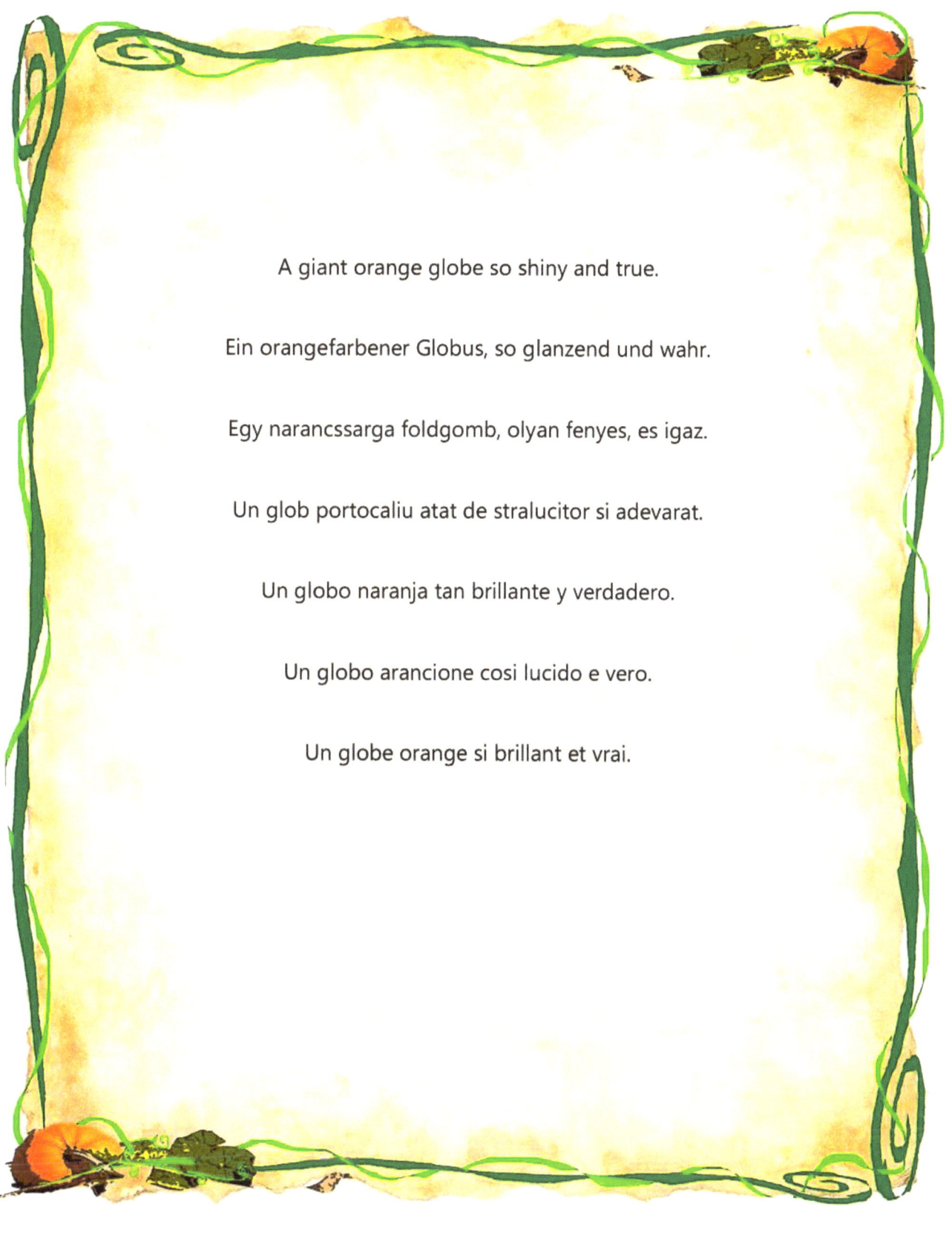

A giant orange globe so shiny and true.

Ein orangefarbener Globus, so glanzend und wahr.

Egy narancssarga foldgomb, olyan fenyes, es igaz.

Un glob portocaliu atat de stralucitor si adevarat.

Un globo naranja tan brillante y verdadero.

Un globo arancione cosi lucido e vero.

Un globe orange si brillant et vrai.

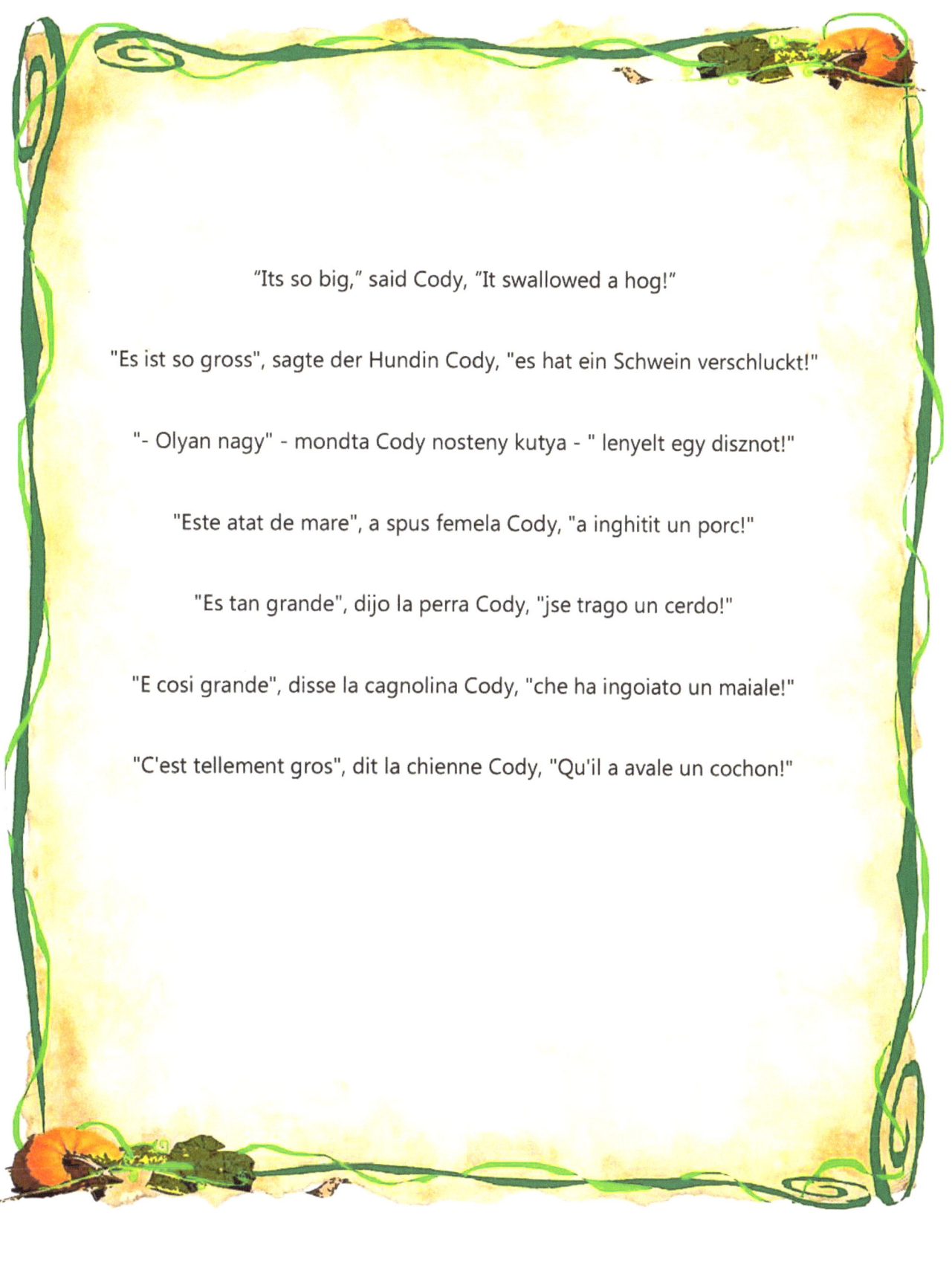

"Its so big," said Cody, "It swallowed a hog!"

"Es ist so gross", sagte der Hundin Cody, "es hat ein Schwein verschluckt!"

"- Olyan nagy" - mondta Cody nosteny kutya - " lenyelt egy disznot!"

"Este atat de mare", a spus femela Cody, "a inghitit un porc!"

"Es tan grande", dijo la perra Cody, "jse trago un cerdo!"

"E cosi grande", disse la cagnolina Cody, "che ha ingoiato un maiale!"

"C'est tellement gros", dit la chienne Cody, "Qu'il a avale un cochon!"

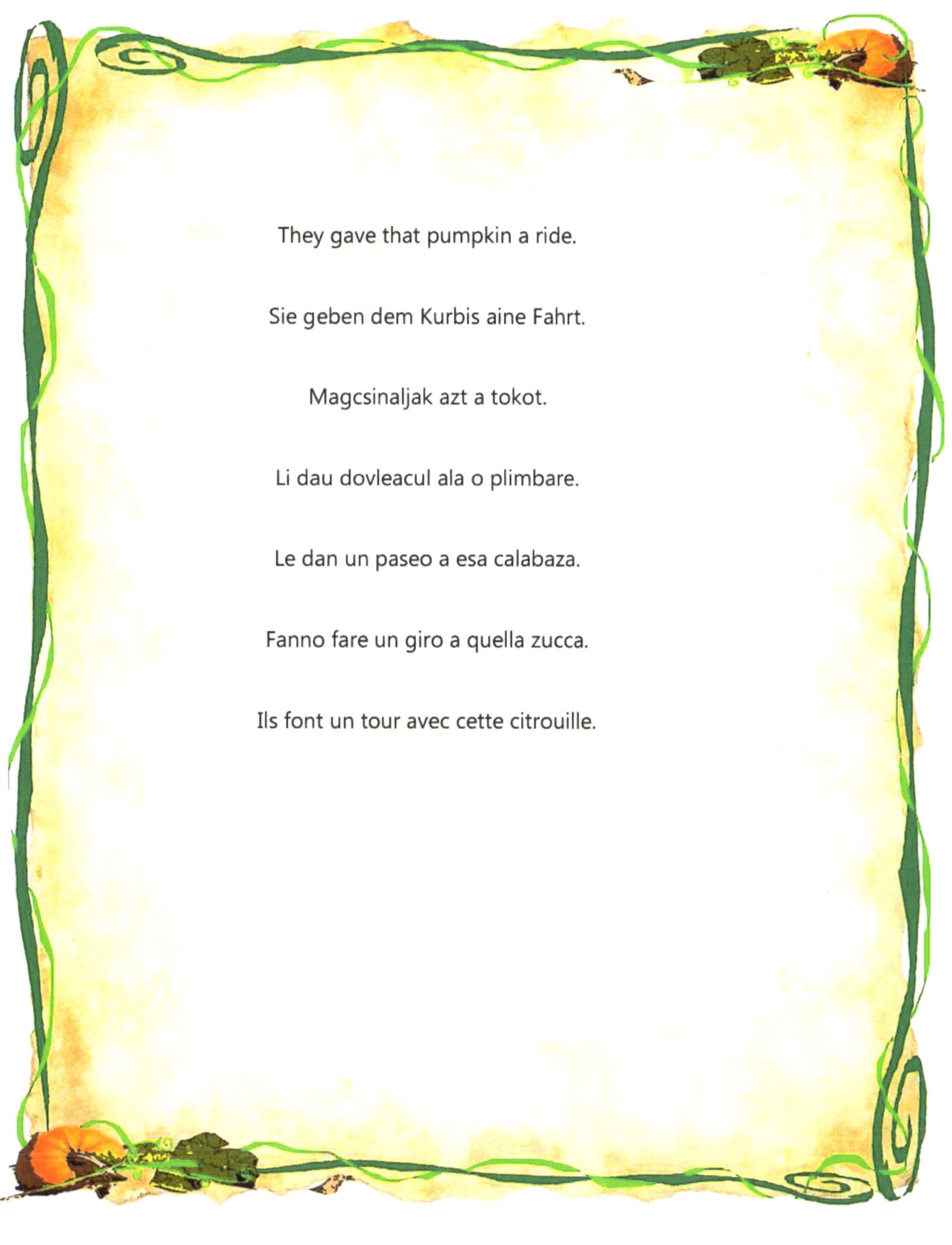

They gave that pumpkin a ride.

Sie geben dem Kurbis aine Fahrt.

Magcsinaljak azt a tokot.

Li dau dovleacul ala o plimbare.

Le dan un paseo a esa calabaza.

Fanno fare un giro a quella zucca.

Ils font un tour avec cette citrouille.

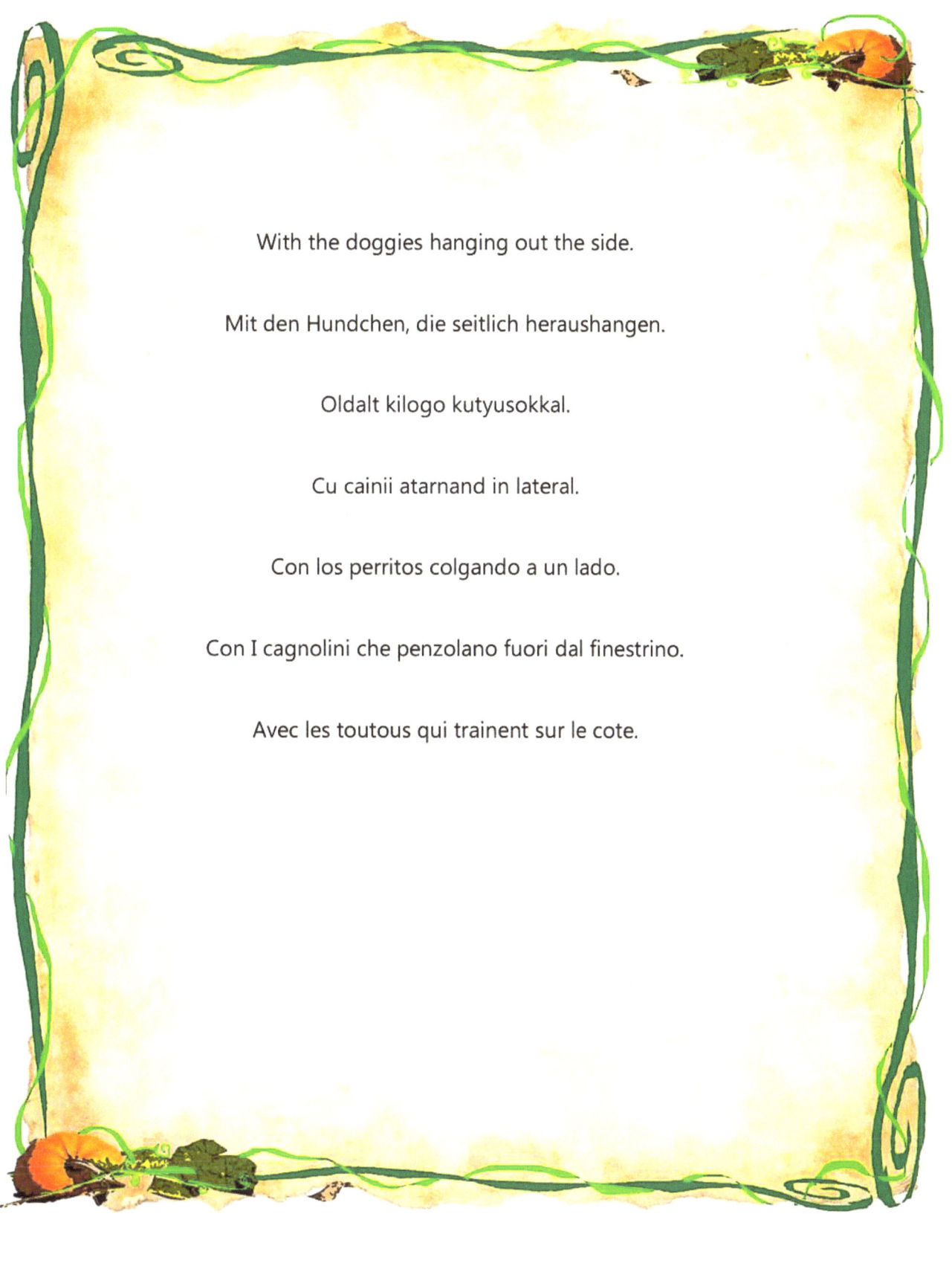

With the doggies hanging out the side.

Mit den Hundchen, die seitlich heraushangen.

Oldalt kilogo kutyusokkal.

Cu cainii atarnand in lateral.

Con los perritos colgando a un lado.

Con I cagnolini che penzolano fuori dal finestrino.

Avec les toutous qui trainent sur le cote.

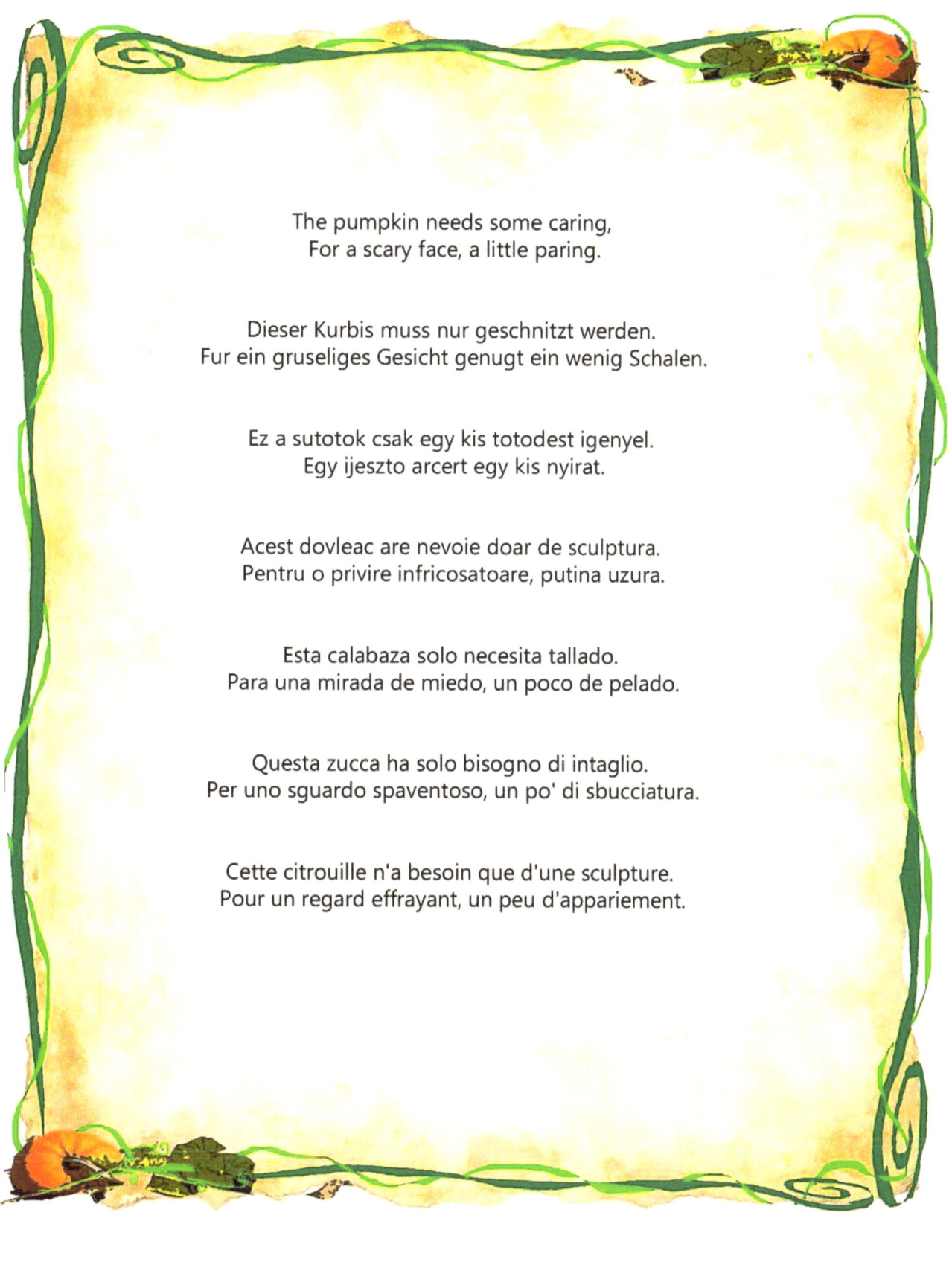

The pumpkin needs some caring,
For a scary face, a little paring.

Dieser Kurbis muss nur geschnitzt werden.
Fur ein gruseliges Gesicht genugt ein wenig Schalen.

Ez a sutotok csak egy kis totodest igenyel.
Egy ijeszto arcert egy kis nyirat.

Acest dovleac are nevoie doar de sculptura.
Pentru o privire infricosatoare, putina uzura.

Esta calabaza solo necesita tallado.
Para una mirada de miedo, un poco de pelado.

Questa zucca ha solo bisogno di intaglio.
Per uno sguardo spaventoso, un po' di sbucciatura.

Cette citrouille n'a besoin que d'une sculpture.
Pour un regard effrayant, un peu d'appariement.

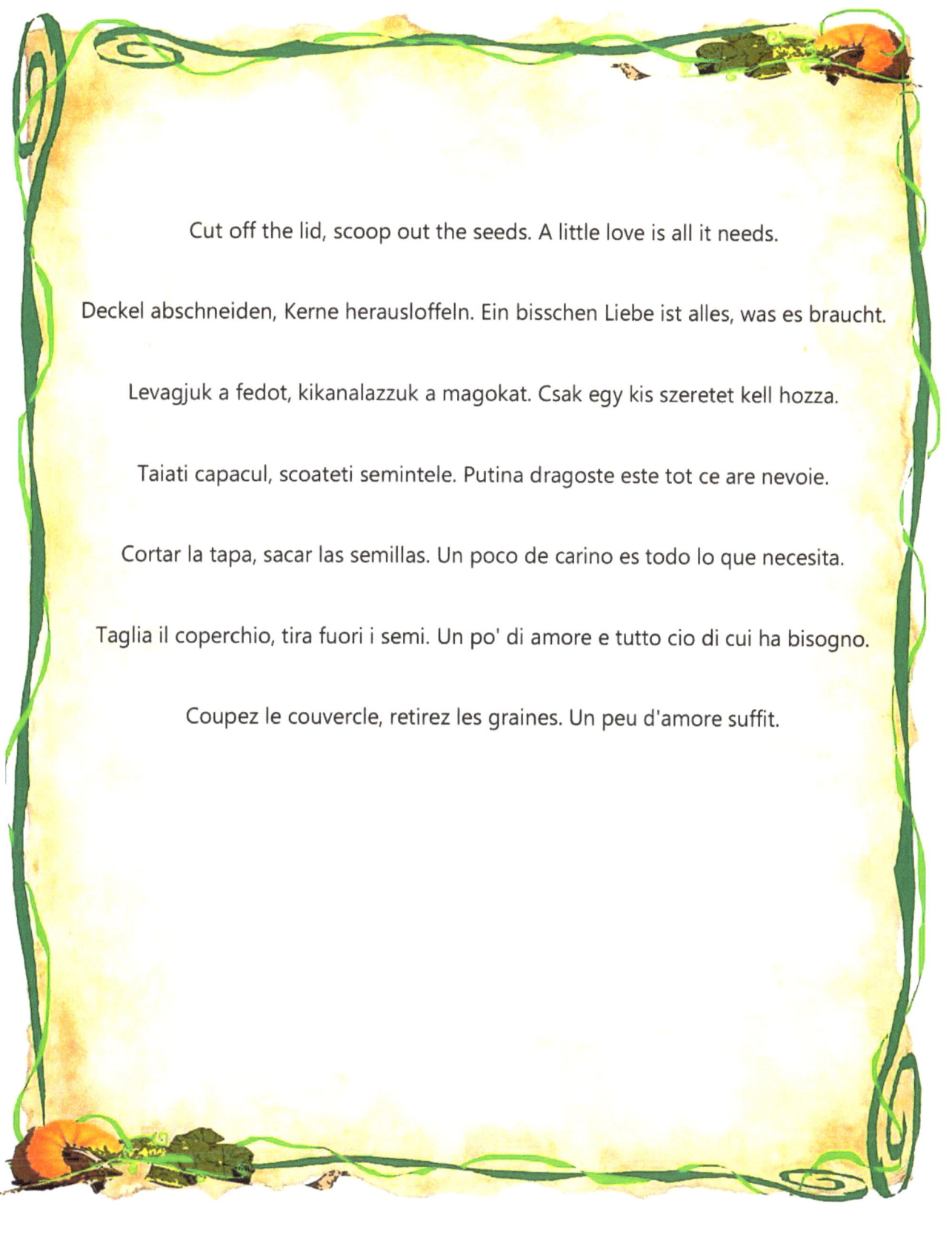

Cut off the lid, scoop out the seeds. A little love is all it needs.

Deckel abschneiden, Kerne herausloffeln. Ein bisschen Liebe ist alles, was es braucht.

Levagjuk a fedot, kikanalazzuk a magokat. Csak egy kis szeretet kell hozza.

Taiati capacul, scoateti semintele. Putina dragoste este tot ce are nevoie.

Cortar la tapa, sacar las semillas. Un poco de carino es todo lo que necesita.

Taglia il coperchio, tira fuori i semi. Un po' di amore e tutto cio di cui ha bisogno.

Coupez le couvercle, retirez les graines. Un peu d'amore suffit.

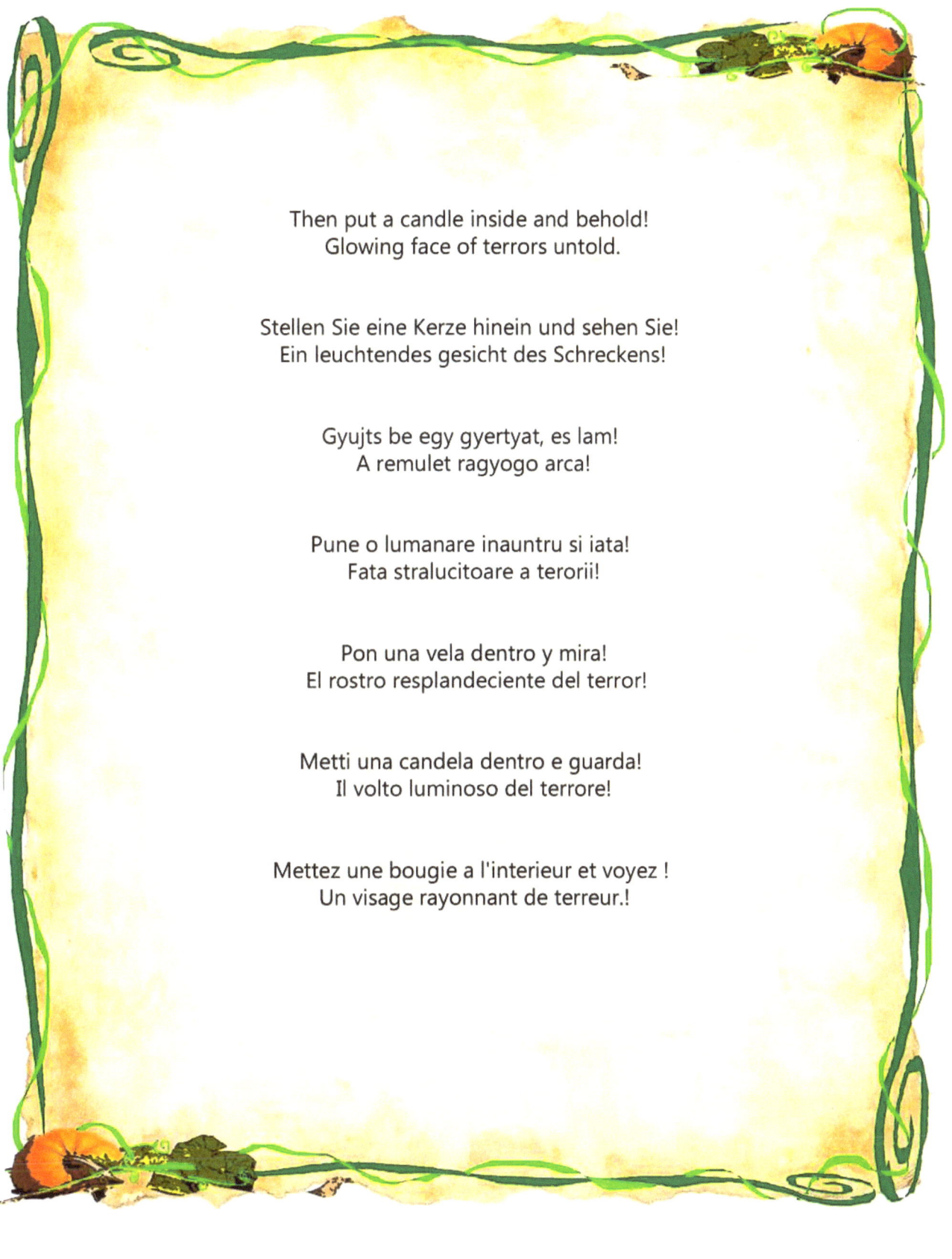

Then put a candle inside and behold!
Glowing face of terrors untold.

Stellen Sie eine Kerze hinein und sehen Sie!
Ein leuchtendes gesicht des Schreckens!

Gyujts be egy gyertyat, es lam!
A remulet ragyogo arca!

Pune o lumanare inauntru si iata!
Fata stralucitoare a terorii!

Pon una vela dentro y mira!
El rostro resplandeciente del terror!

Metti una candela dentro e guarda!
Il volto luminoso del terrore!

Mettez une bougie a l'interieur et voyez !
Un visage rayonnant de terreur.!

Flickering eyes and grin of dread,
tells the story of ghosts un-dead.

Flackernde Augen und Todesgrinsen
erzahlen eine Geschichte von untoten Geistern.

Villodzo szemek es halalvigyor,
elohalott szellemek tortenetet meseli el.

Ochii palpaitori si ranjetul mortii,
spune o poveste despre fantome strigoi.

Ojos parpadeantes y sonrisa de muete,
cuenta una historia de fantasmas no muertos.

Occhi tremolanti e un ghigno mortale
raccontano una storia di fantasmi non morti.

Des yeux scintillants et un sourire mortel
racontent une histoire de fantomes morts-vivants.

"Use the broom, not the mop!"
She ties the pointy black hat right on top.

"Benutze den Besen, nicht den Wischmopp!"
Sie bindet sich einen spitzen schwartzen Hut auf den kopf.

-A sepreut hasznald, ne a fel mosot!
Pontosan a fejere kot egy hegyes fekete kalapot.

"Foloseste matura, nu mopul!"
Isi leaga o palarie neagra ascutita chiar pe cap.

"Usa la escoba, no el, trapeador!"
Se ata un sombrero negro puntiaundo en la cabeza.

"Usa la scopa, nonlo straccio!"
Si lega un cappello nero a punta direttamente in testa.

"Utilise le balai et non la serpillere !"
Elle attache un chapeau noir pointu sur sa tete.

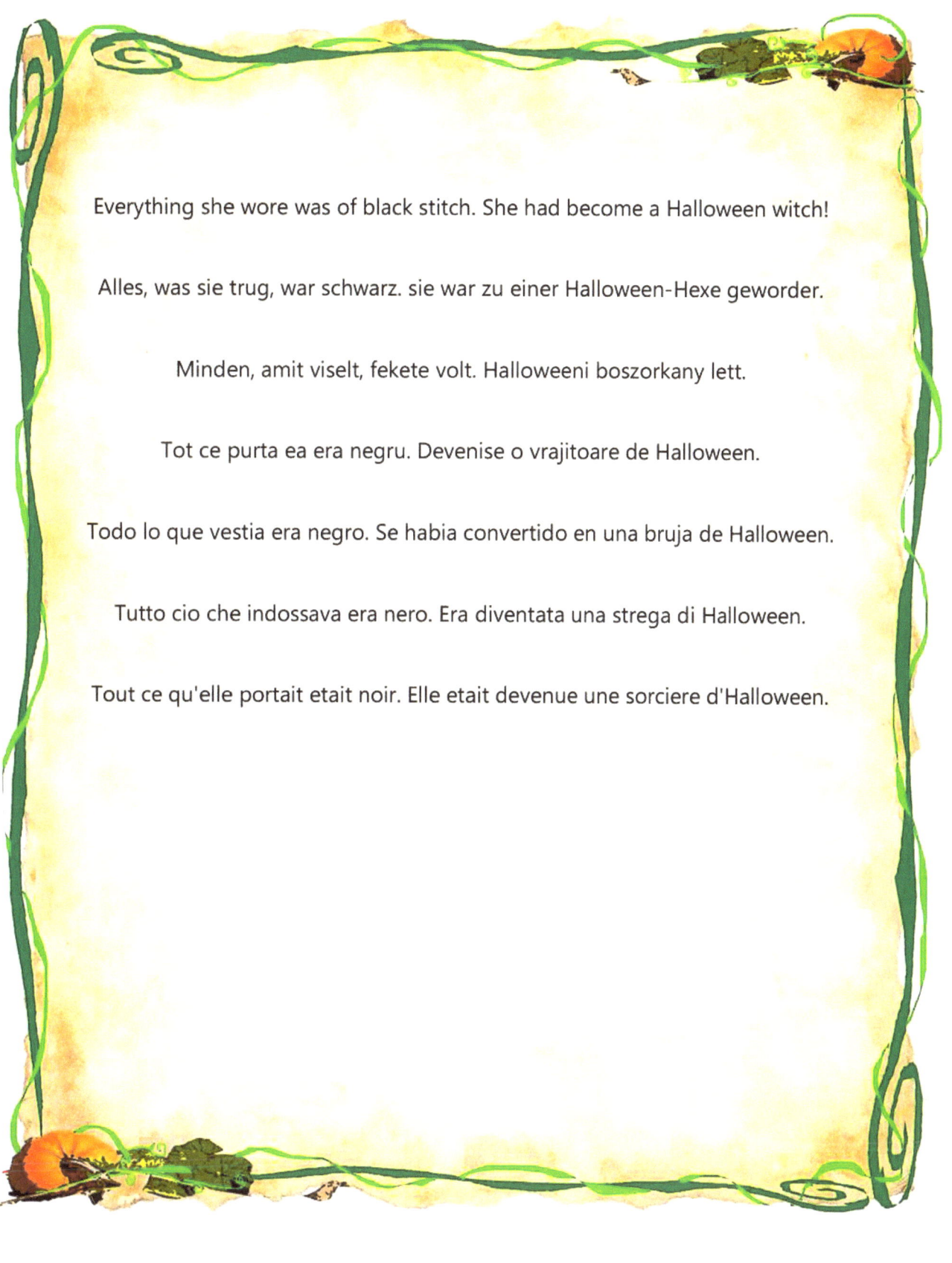

Everything she wore was of black stitch. She had become a Halloween witch!

Alles, was sie trug, war schwarz. sie war zu einer Halloween-Hexe geworder.

Minden, amit viselt, fekete volt. Halloweeni boszorkany lett.

Tot ce purta ea era negru. Devenise o vrajitoare de Halloween.

Todo lo que vestia era negro. Se habia convertido en una bruja de Halloween.

Tutto cio che indossava era nero. Era diventata una strega di Halloween.

Tout ce qu'elle portait etait noir. Elle etait devenue une sorciere d'Halloween.

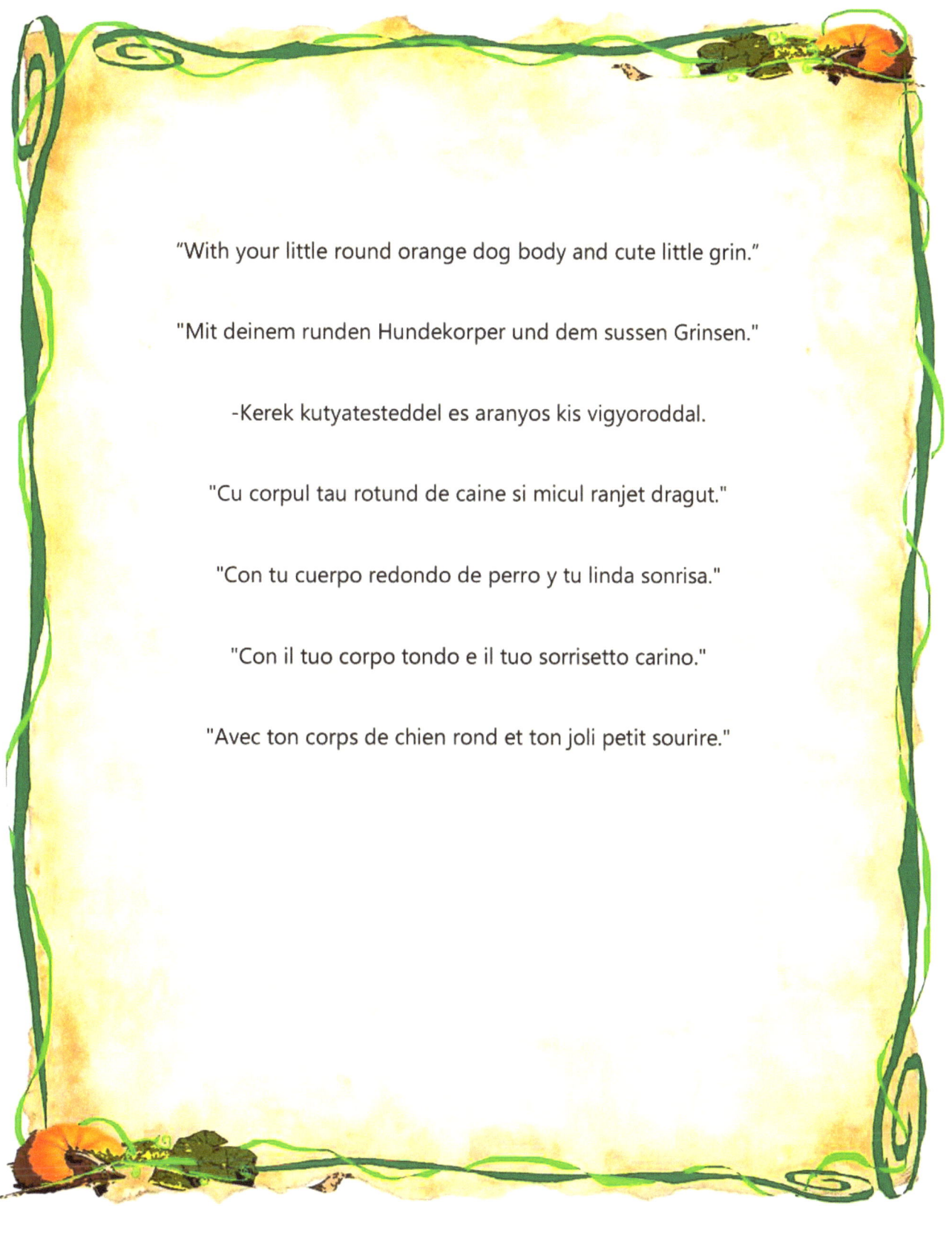

"With your little round orange dog body and cute little grin."

"Mit deinem runden Hundekorper und dem sussen Grinsen."

-Kerek kutyatesteddel es aranyos kis vigyoroddal.

"Cu corpul tau rotund de caine si micul ranjet dragut."

"Con tu cuerpo redondo de perro y tu linda sonrisa."

"Con il tuo corpo tondo e il tuo sorrisetto carino."

"Avec ton corps de chien rond et ton joli petit sourire."

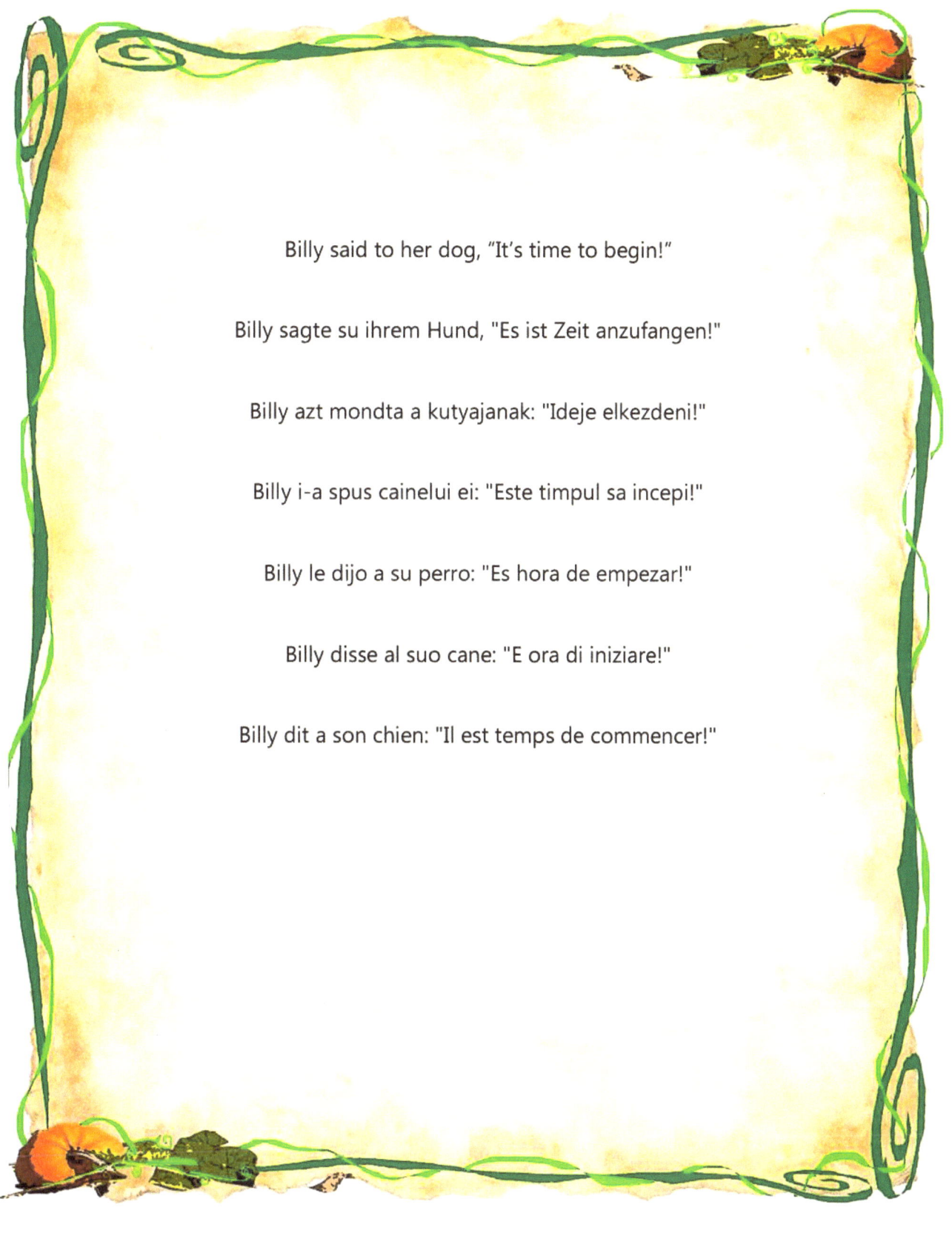

Billy said to her dog, "It's time to begin!"

Billy sagte su ihrem Hund, "Es ist Zeit anzufangen!"

Billy azt mondta a kutyajanak: "Ideje elkezdeni!"

Billy i-a spus cainelui ei: "Este timpul sa incepi!"

Billy le dijo a su perro: "Es hora de empezar!"

Billy disse al suo cane: "E ora di iniziare!"

Billy dit a son chien: "Il est temps de commencer!"

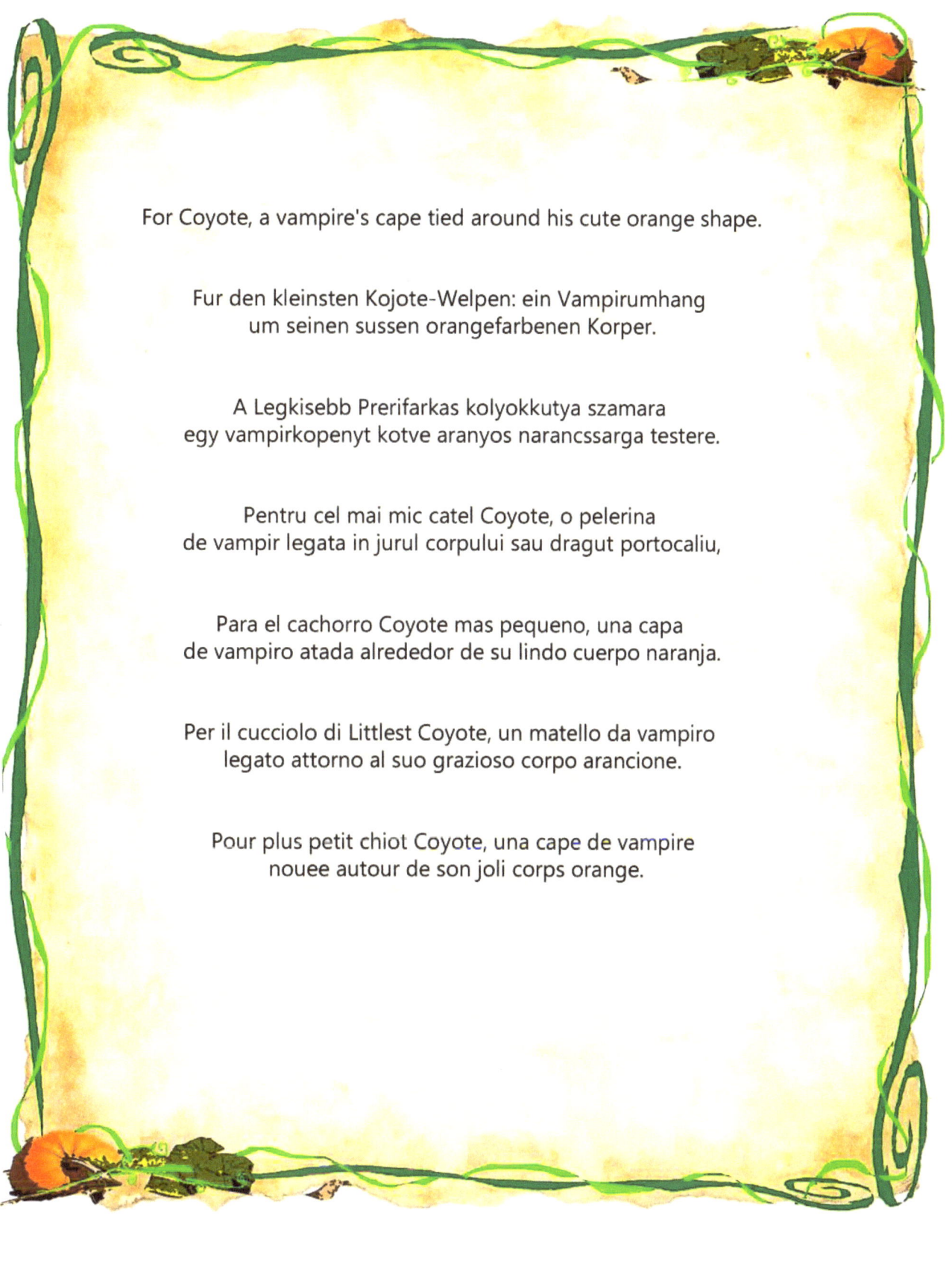

For Coyote, a vampire's cape tied around his cute orange shape.

Fur den kleinsten Kojote-Welpen: ein Vampirumhang
um seinen sussen orangefarbenen Korper.

A Legkisebb Prerifarkas kolyokkutya szamara
egy vampirkopenyt kotve aranyos narancssarga testere.

Pentru cel mai mic catel Coyote, o pelerina
de vampir legata in jurul corpului sau dragut portocaliu,

Para el cachorro Coyote mas pequeno, una capa
de vampiro atada alrededor de su lindo cuerpo naranja.

Per il cucciolo di Littlest Coyote, un matello da vampiro
legato attorno al suo grazioso corpo arancione.

Pour plus petit chiot Coyote, una cape de vampire
nouee autour de son joli corps orange.

"What am I?" said the puppy, pumpkin seeds in his fur.
"The Littlest Vampire, that's for sure!"

"Was bin ich?" heulte der Hund, kurbiskerne steckten in seinem Fell,
"Der kleinste Vampir, das ist sicher!"

-Mi vagyok en? uvoltott a kutya, tokmagok ragdtak a bundejaba.
"A legkisebb vampir, as biztos!"

"Ce sunt eu?" urla cainele, cu semintele de dovleac infipte in blana.
"Cel mai mic vampir, asta e sigur!"

"Que soy yo?" aullo el perro con semillas de calabaza pegada en su pelaje.
"El vampira mas pequeno, eso es seguro!"

"Cosa sono?" ululo il cane, con i semi do zucca incatrati nella pelliccia.
"Il piu piccolo vampiro, questo e sicuro!"

"Que suis-je ?" hurla le chein, des graines de citrouille coincees dans sa fourrure.
"Le plus petit vampire, c'est sur!"

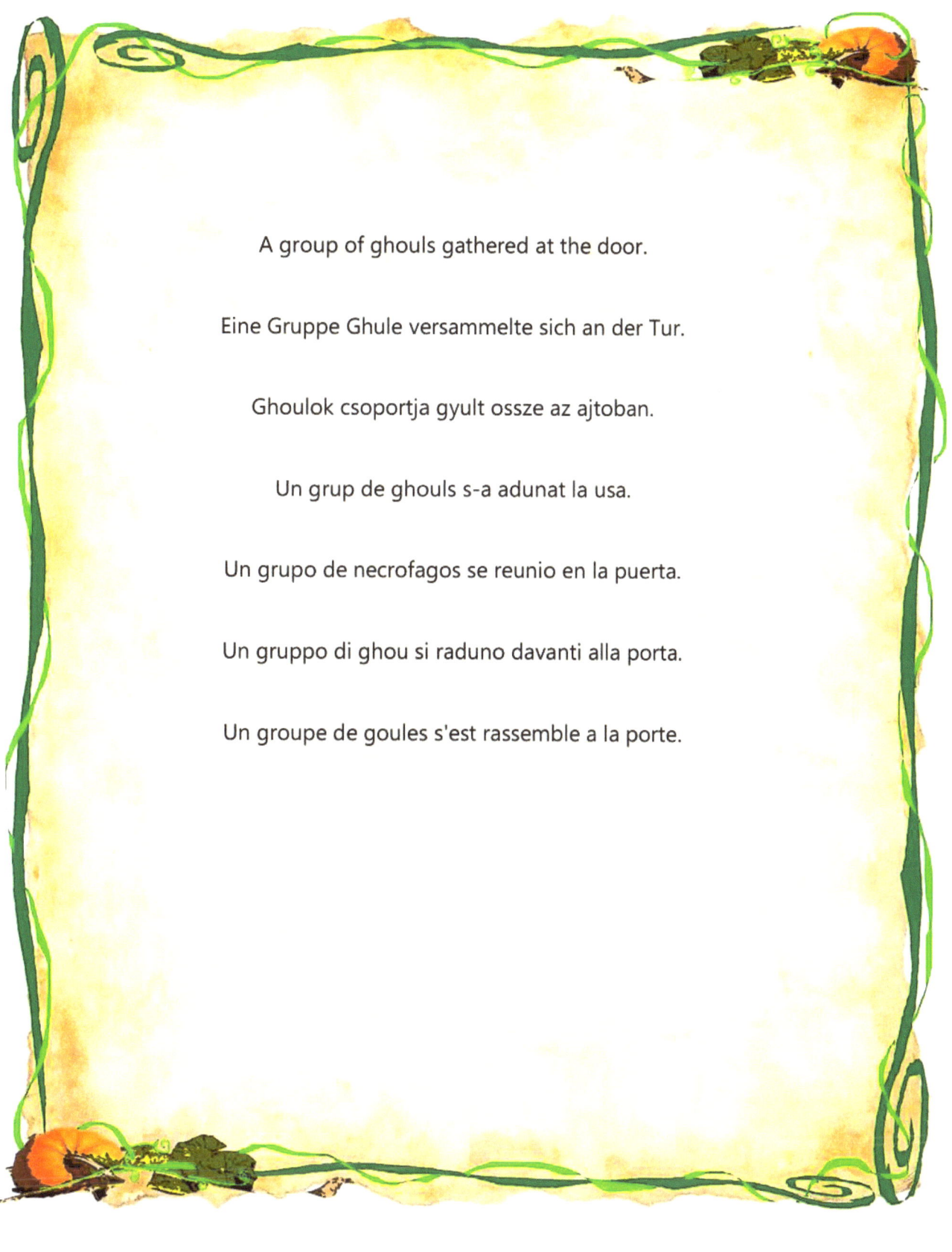

A group of ghouls gathered at the door.

Eine Gruppe Ghule versammelte sich an der Tur.

Ghoulok csoportja gyult ossze az ajtoban.

Un grup de ghouls s-a adunat la usa.

Un grupo de necrofagos se reunio en la puerta.

Un gruppo di ghou si raduno davanti alla porta.

Un groupe de goules s'est rassemble a la porte.

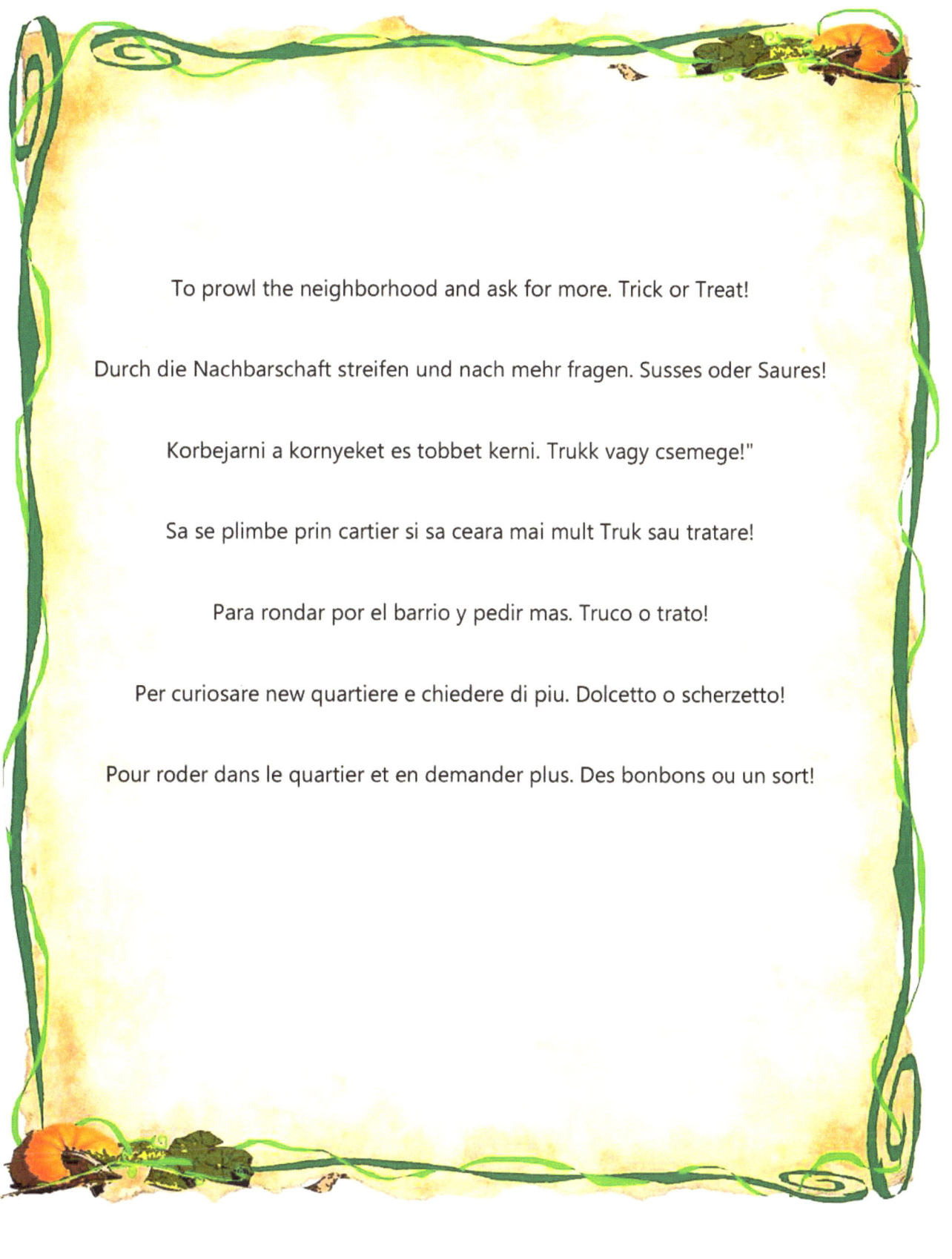

To prowl the neighborhood and ask for more. Trick or Treat!

Durch die Nachbarschaft streifen und nach mehr fragen. Susses oder Saures!

Korbejarni a kornyeket es tobbet kerni. Trukk vagy csemege!"

Sa se plimbe prin cartier si sa ceara mai mult Truk sau tratare!

Para rondar por el barrio y pedir mas. Truco o trato!

Per curiosare new quartiere e chiedere di piu. Dolcetto o scherzetto!

Pour roder dans le quartier et en demander plus. Des bonbons ou un sort!

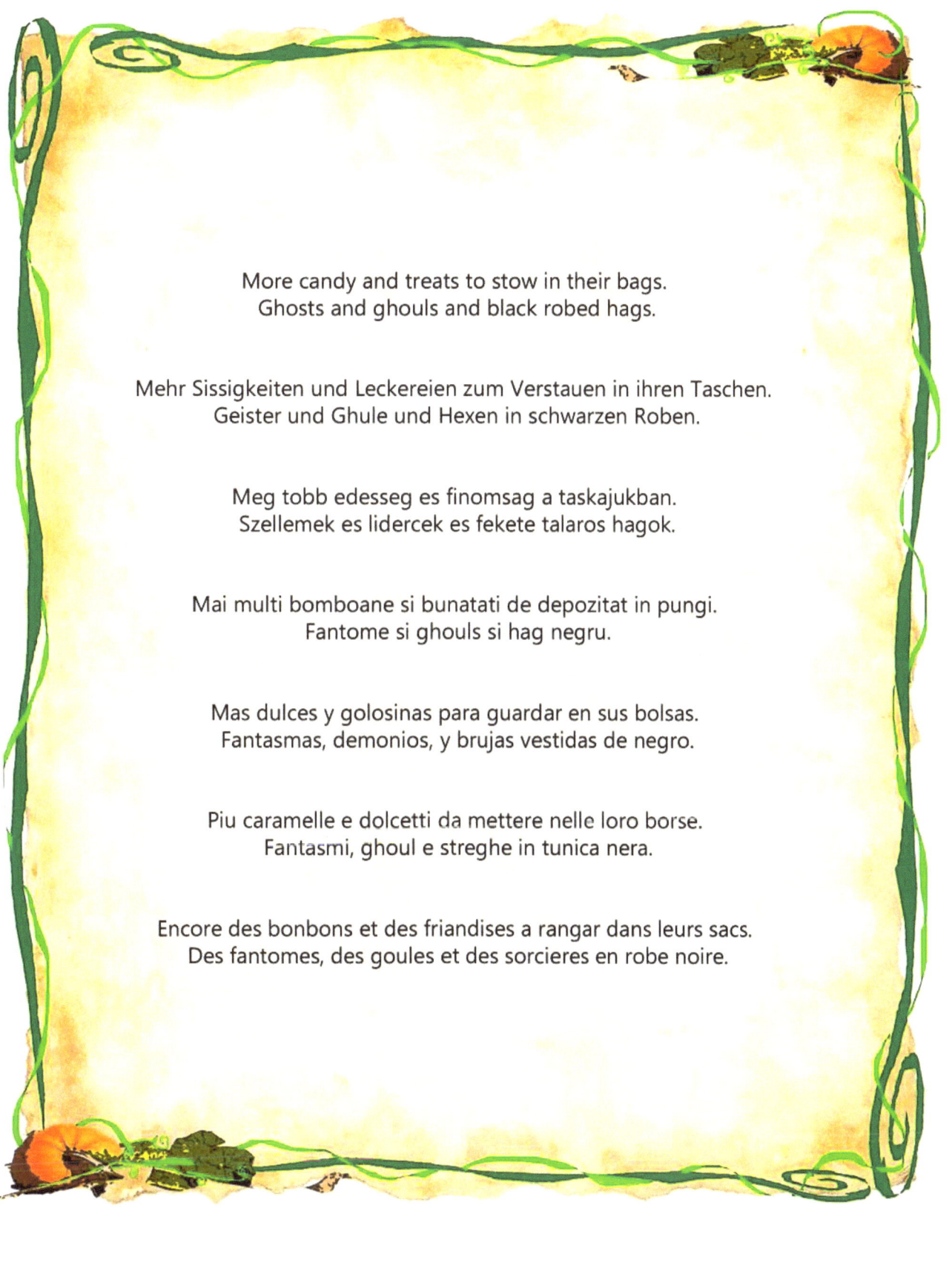

More candy and treats to stow in their bags.
Ghosts and ghouls and black robed hags.

Mehr Sissigkeiten und Leckereien zum Verstauen in ihren Taschen.
Geister und Ghule und Hexen in schwarzen Roben.

Meg tobb edesseg es finomsag a taskajukban.
Szellemek es lidercek es fekete talaros hagok.

Mai multi bomboane si bunatati de depozitat in pungi.
Fantome si ghouls si hag negru.

Mas dulces y golosinas para guardar en sus bolsas.
Fantasmas, demonios, y brujas vestidas de negro.

Piu caramelle e dolcetti da mettere nelle loro borse.
Fantasmi, ghoul e streghe in tunica nera.

Encore des bonbons et des friandises a rangar dans leurs sacs.
Des fantomes, des goules et des sorcieres en robe noire.

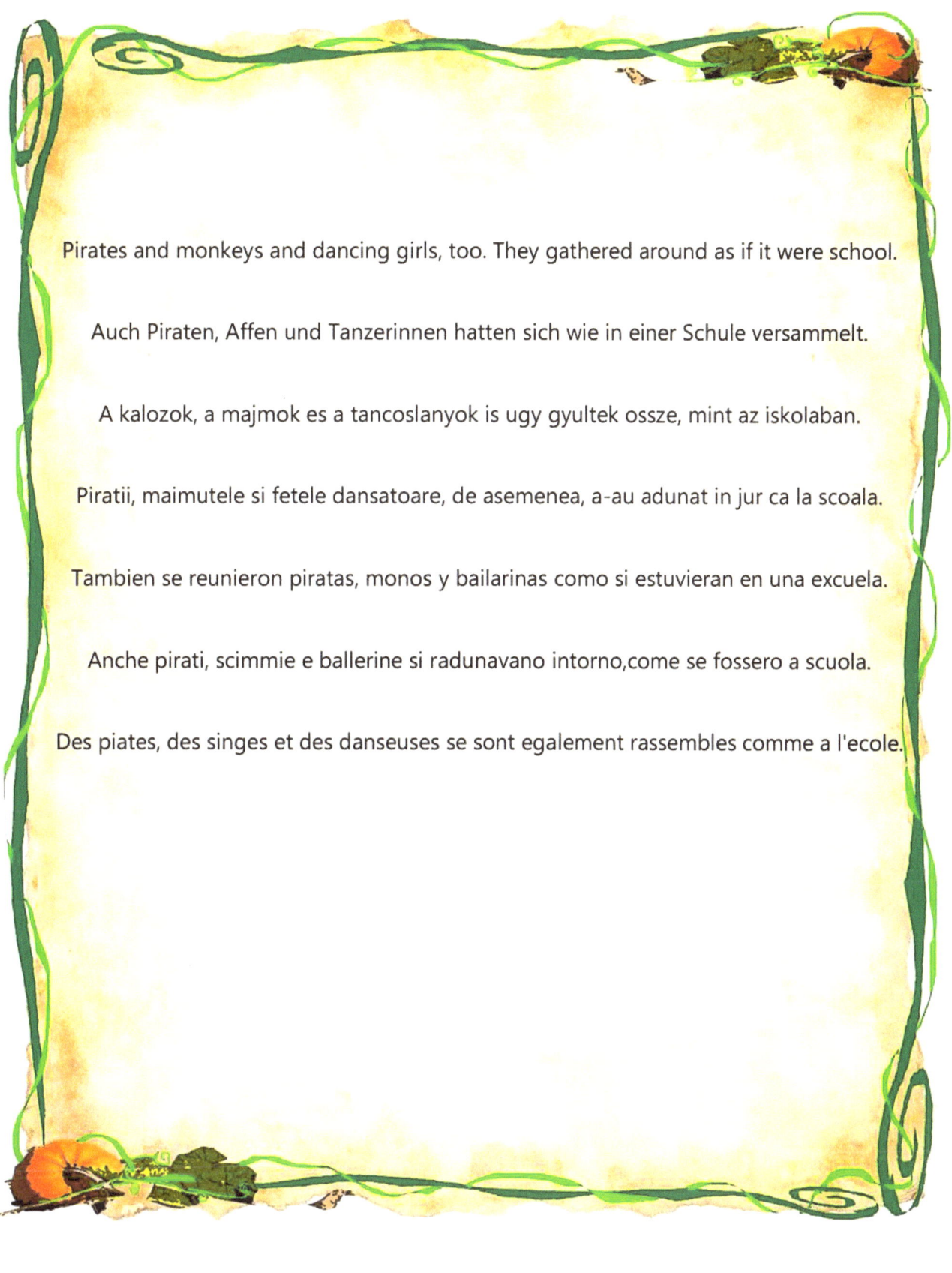

Pirates and monkeys and dancing girls, too. They gathered around as if it were school.

Auch Piraten, Affen und Tanzerinnen hatten sich wie in einer Schule versammelt.

A kalozok, a majmok es a tancoslanyok is ugy gyultek ossze, mint az iskolaban.

Piratii, maimutele si fetele dansatoare, de asemenea, a-au adunat in jur ca la scoala.

Tambien se reunieron piratas, monos y bailarinas como si estuvieran en una excuela.

Anche pirati, scimmie e ballerine si radunavano intorno,come se fossero a scuola.

Des piates, des singes et des danseuses se sont egalement rassembles comme a l'ecole.

"Trick or Treat!" they called at each door,
holding up bags begging for more.

"Susses oder Saures?" riefen sie an jeder Tur
und hielten Tuten hoch, um um mehr zu betteln.

Trukk vagy csemege? Minden ajtonal kiabaltak,
es feltartottak a taskakat, hogy tobbert.

Truc sau tratare? Strigau la fiecare use tinand
pungi in sus ca sa cerseasca mai mult.

Truco o trato? Gritaban en cada puerta,
levantando bolsas para pedir mas.

Dolcetto o scherzetto? Si presentavano a ogni porta,
reggendo le borse per chiedere di piu.

Des bonbons ou un sort? Ils ont appele a chaque porte,
brandissant des sacs pour en demaner.

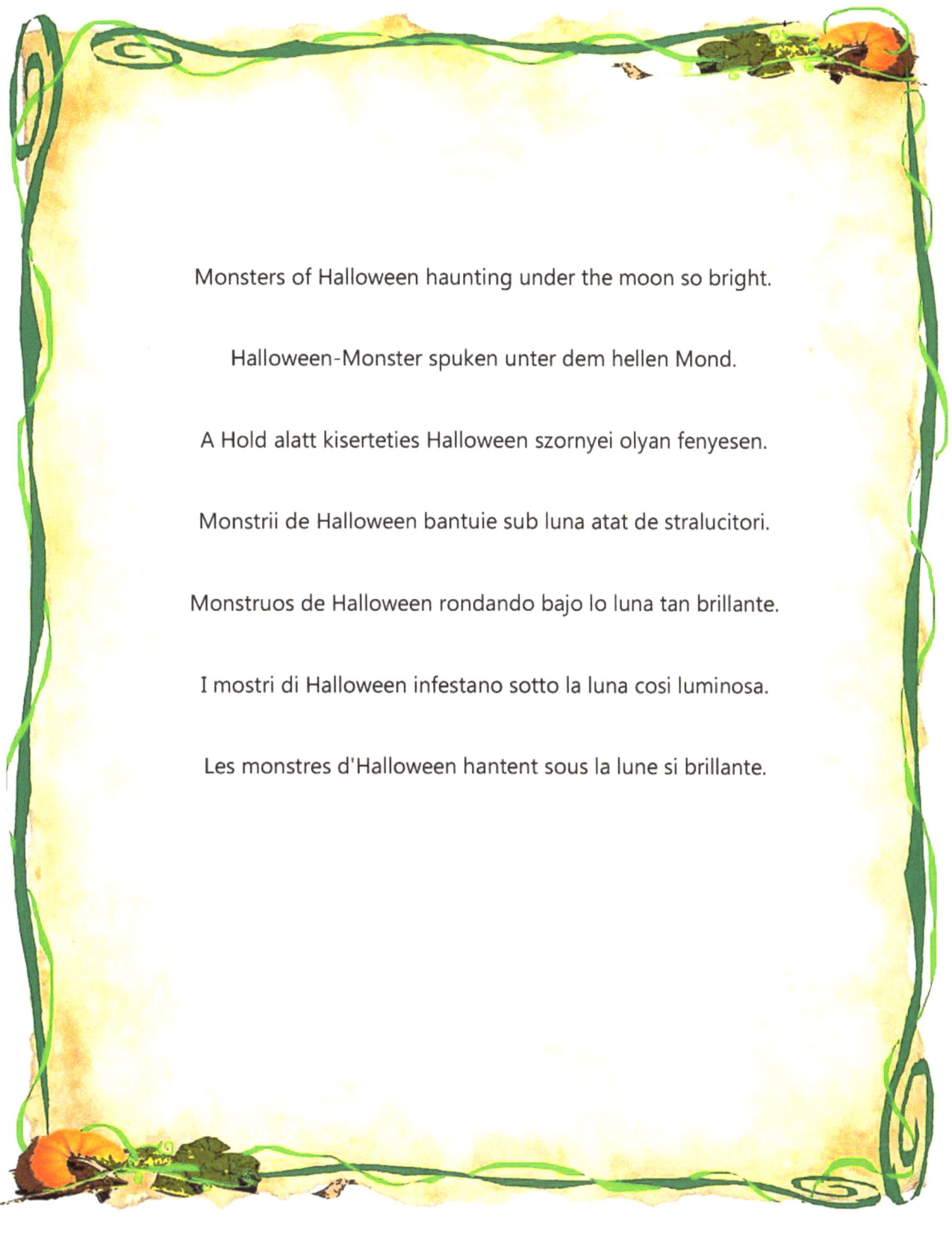

Monsters of Halloween haunting under the moon so bright.

Halloween-Monster spuken unter dem hellen Mond.

A Hold alatt kiserteties Halloween szornyei olyan fenyesen.

Monstrii de Halloween bantuie sub luna atat de stralucitori.

Monstruos de Halloween rondando bajo lo luna tan brillante.

I mostri di Halloween infestano sotto la luna cosi luminosa.

Les monstres d'Halloween hantent sous la lune si brillante.

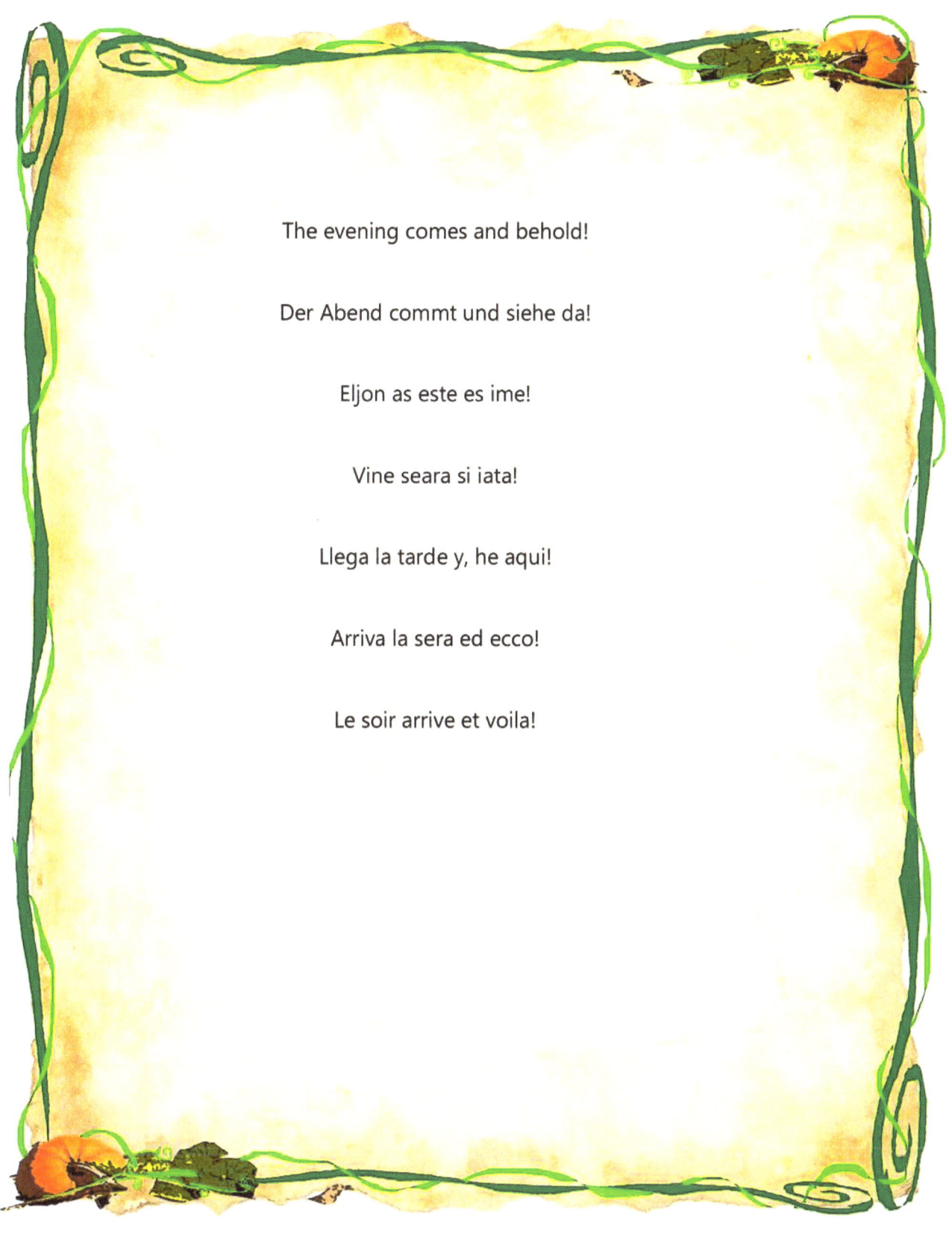

The evening comes and behold!

Der Abend commt und siehe da!

Eljon as este es ime!

Vine seara si iata!

Llega la tarde y, he aqui!

Arriva la sera ed ecco!

Le soir arrive et voila!

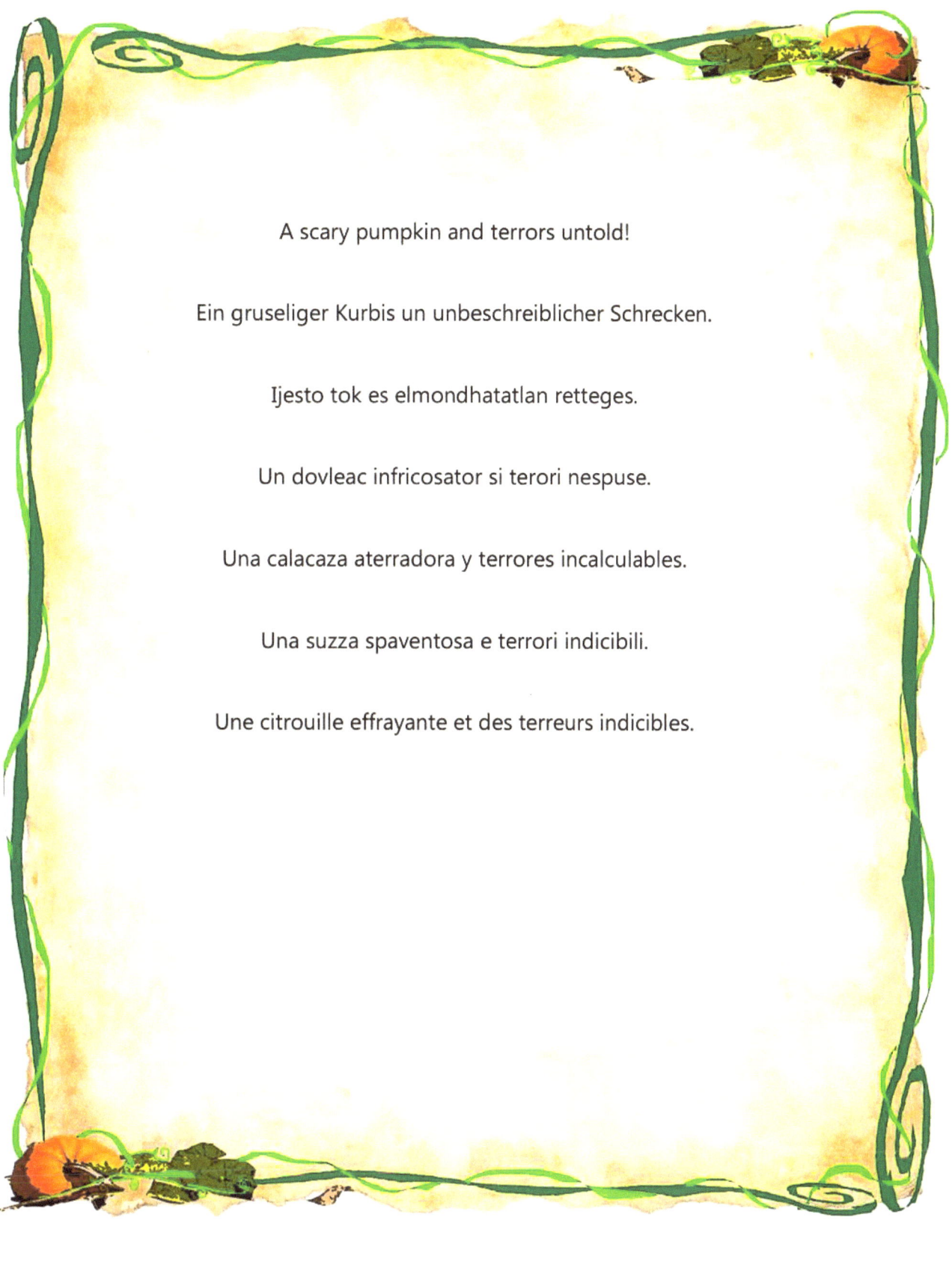

A scary pumpkin and terrors untold!

Ein gruseliger Kurbis un unbeschreiblicher Schrecken.

Ijesto tok es elmondhatatlan retteges.

Un dovleac infricosator si terori nespuse.

Una calacaza aterradora y terrores incalculables.

Una suzza spaventosa e terrori indicibili.

Une citrouille effrayante et des terreurs indicibles.

The big kids came to cause some trouble.

Die grossen Kinder machten Arger.

A nagy gyerekek gondot okoztak.

Copiii mari au venit sa le pese de niste necazuri.

Los ninos mayores vinieron a cousar algunos problemas.

I ragazzi piu grandi sono venuti per combinare qualche guaio.

Les grands enfants sont venus chercher quelques ennuis.

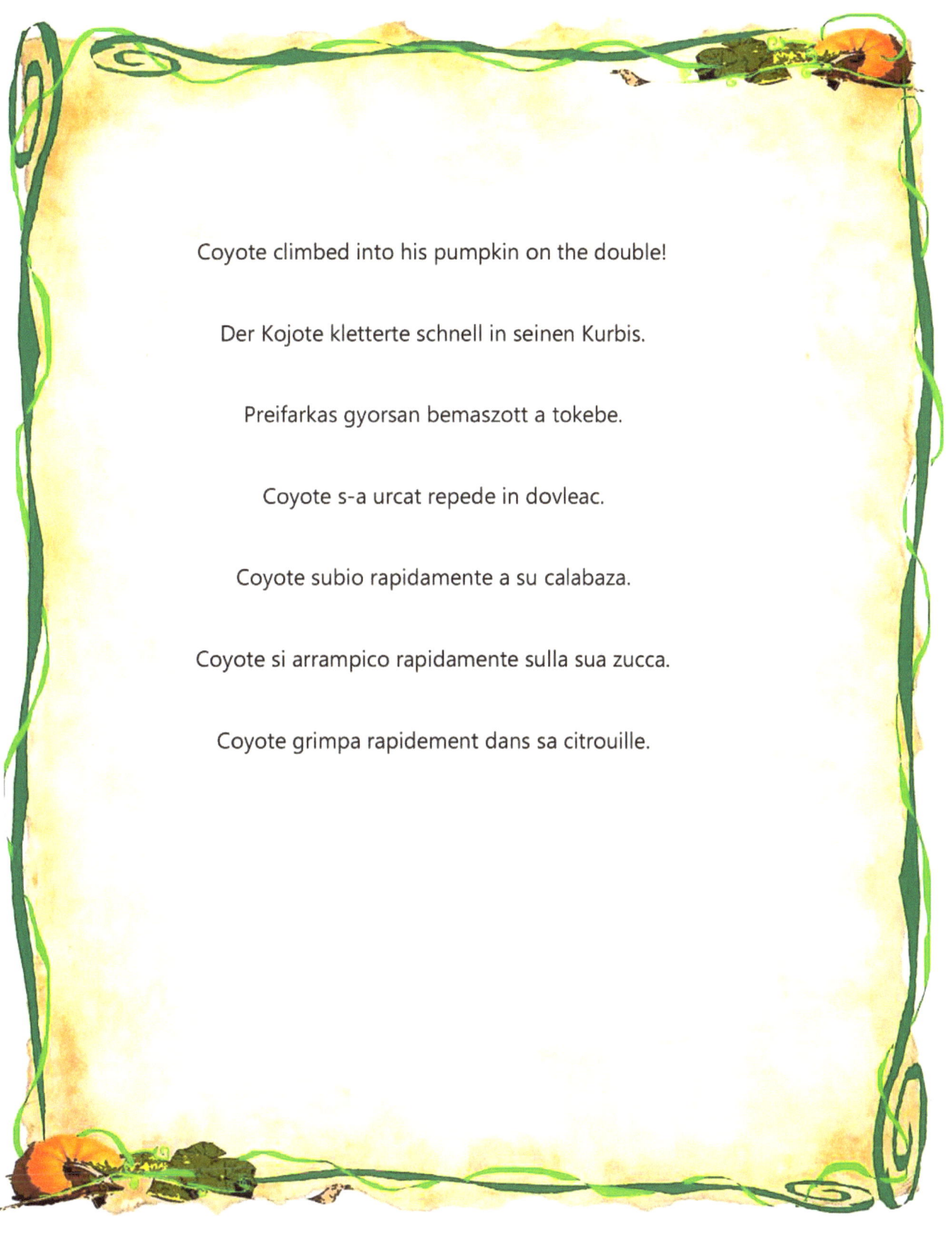

Coyote climbed into his pumpkin on the double!

Der Kojote kletterte schnell in seinen Kurbis.

Preifarkas gyorsan bemaszott a tokebe.

Coyote s-a urcat repede in dovleac.

Coyote subio rapidamente a su calabaza.

Coyote si arrampico rapidamente sulla sua zucca.

Coyote grimpa rapidement dans sa citrouille.

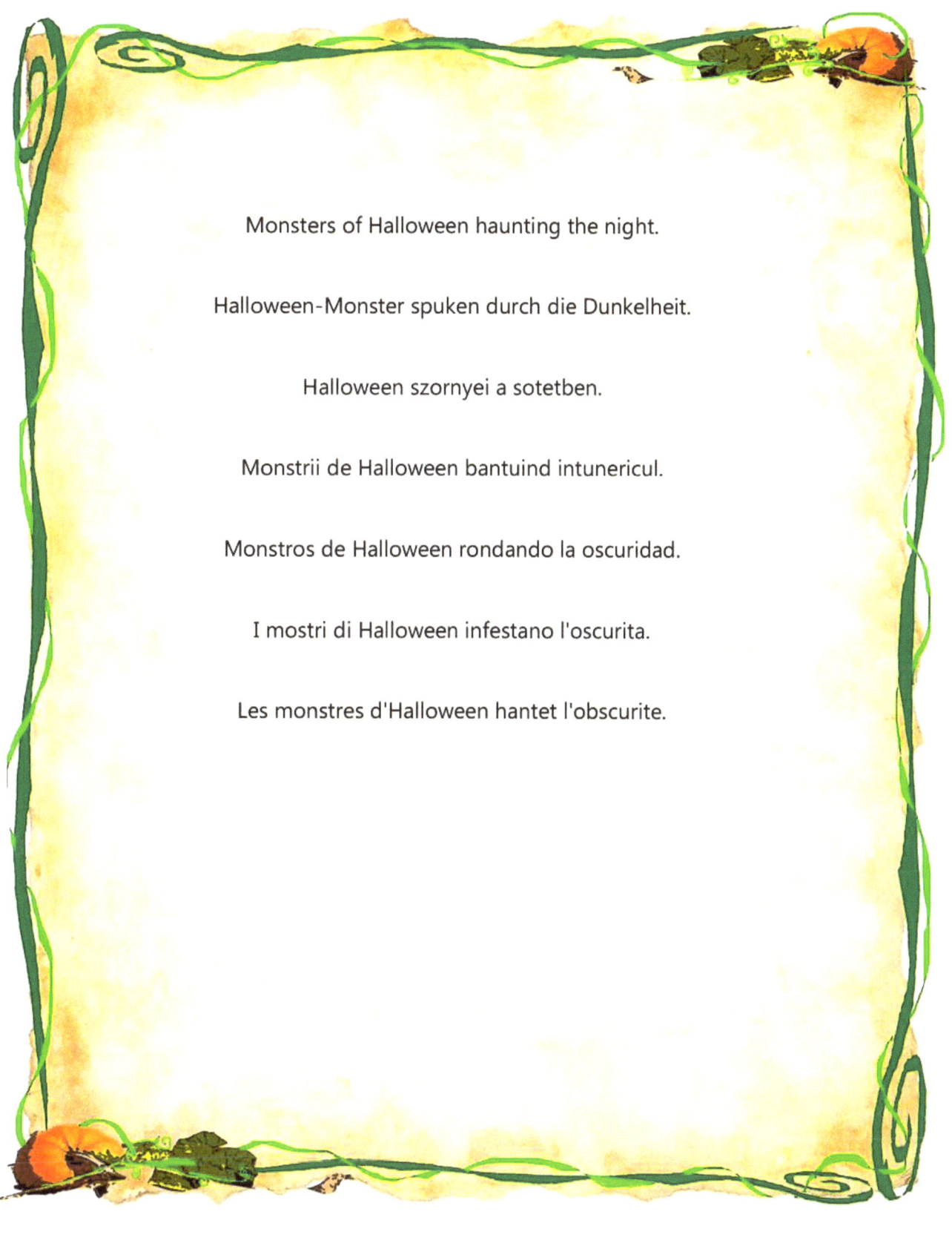

Monsters of Halloween haunting the night.

Halloween-Monster spuken durch die Dunkelheit.

Halloween szornyei a sotetben.

Monstrii de Halloween bantuind intunericul.

Monstros de Halloween rondando la oscuridad.

I mostri di Halloween infestano l'oscurita.

Les monstres d'Halloween hantet l'obscurite.

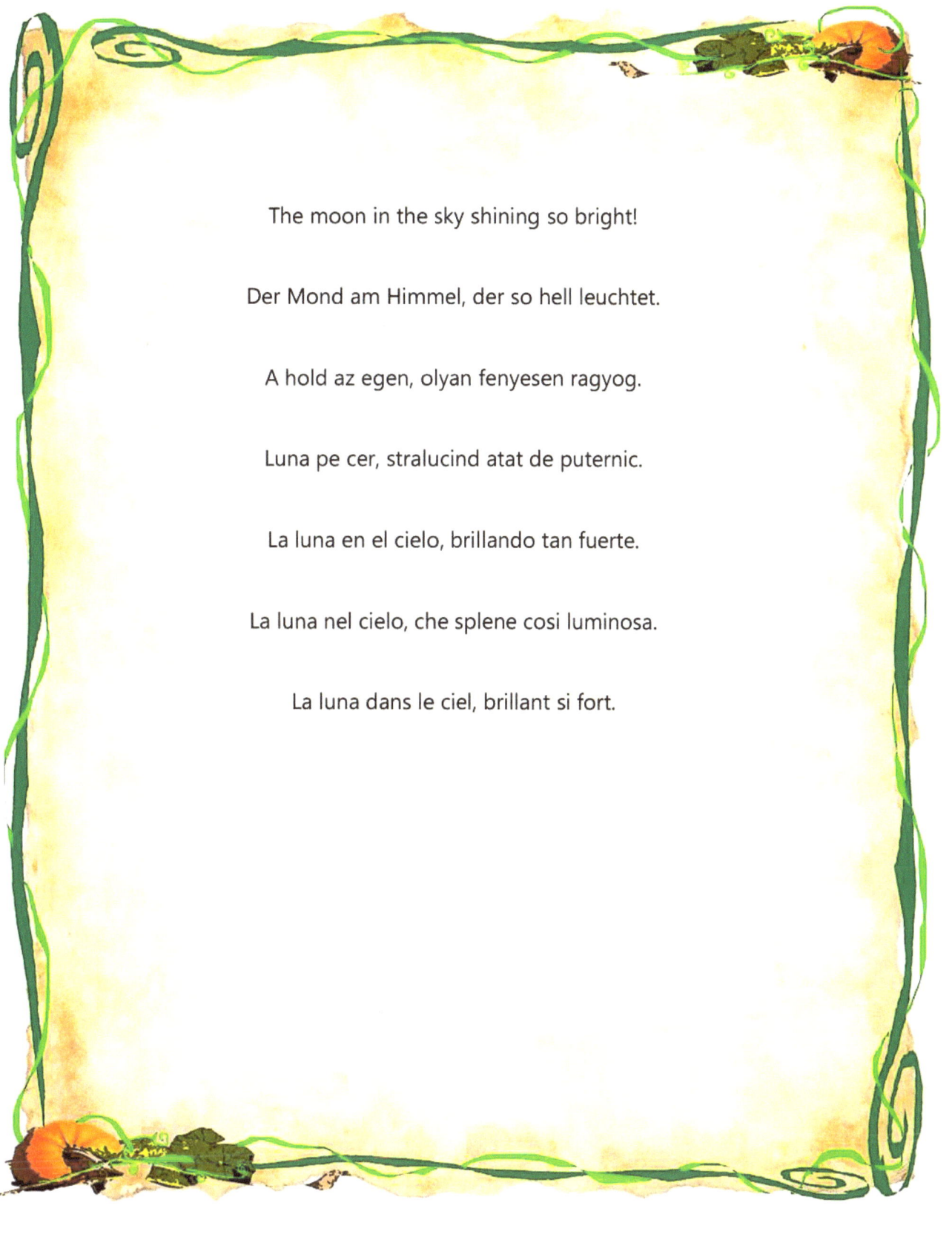

The moon in the sky shining so bright!

Der Mond am Himmel, der so hell leuchtet.

A hold az egen, olyan fenyesen ragyog.

Luna pe cer, stralucind atat de puternic.

La luna en el cielo, brillando tan fuerte.

La luna nel cielo, che splene cosi luminosa.

La luna dans le ciel, brillant si fort.

He pops out of the pumpkin to keep those kids at bay.

Er springt aus seinem Kurbis, um die Kinder fernzuhalten.

Kibujik a tokebol, hogy tavol tartsa azokat a gyerekeket.

Lese din dovleac ca sa-i tina departe pe acei copii.

El sale de su calabaza para mantener a esos ninos alejados.

Esce dalla sua zucca per tenere lontani quei bambini.

Il sort de sa citrouille pour eloigner les enfants

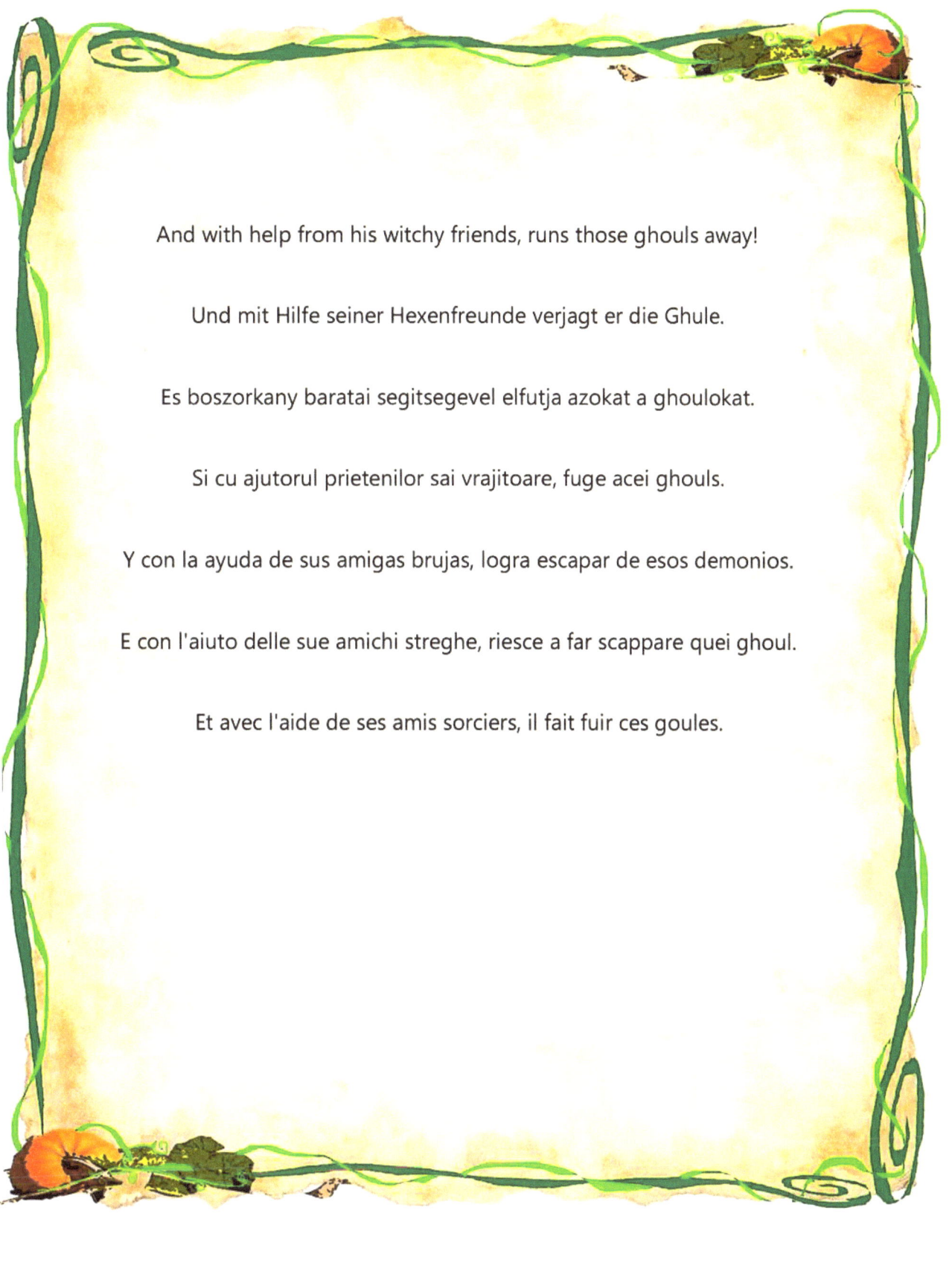

And with help from his witchy friends, runs those ghouls away!

Und mit Hilfe seiner Hexenfreunde verjagt er die Ghule.

Es boszorkany baratai segitsegevel elfutja azokat a ghoulokat.

Si cu ajutorul prietenilor sai vrajitoare, fuge acei ghouls.

Y con la ayuda de sus amigas brujas, logra escapar de esos demonios.

E con l'aiuto delle sue amichi streghe, riesce a far scappare quei ghoul.

Et avec l'aide de ses amis sorciers, il fait fuir ces goules.

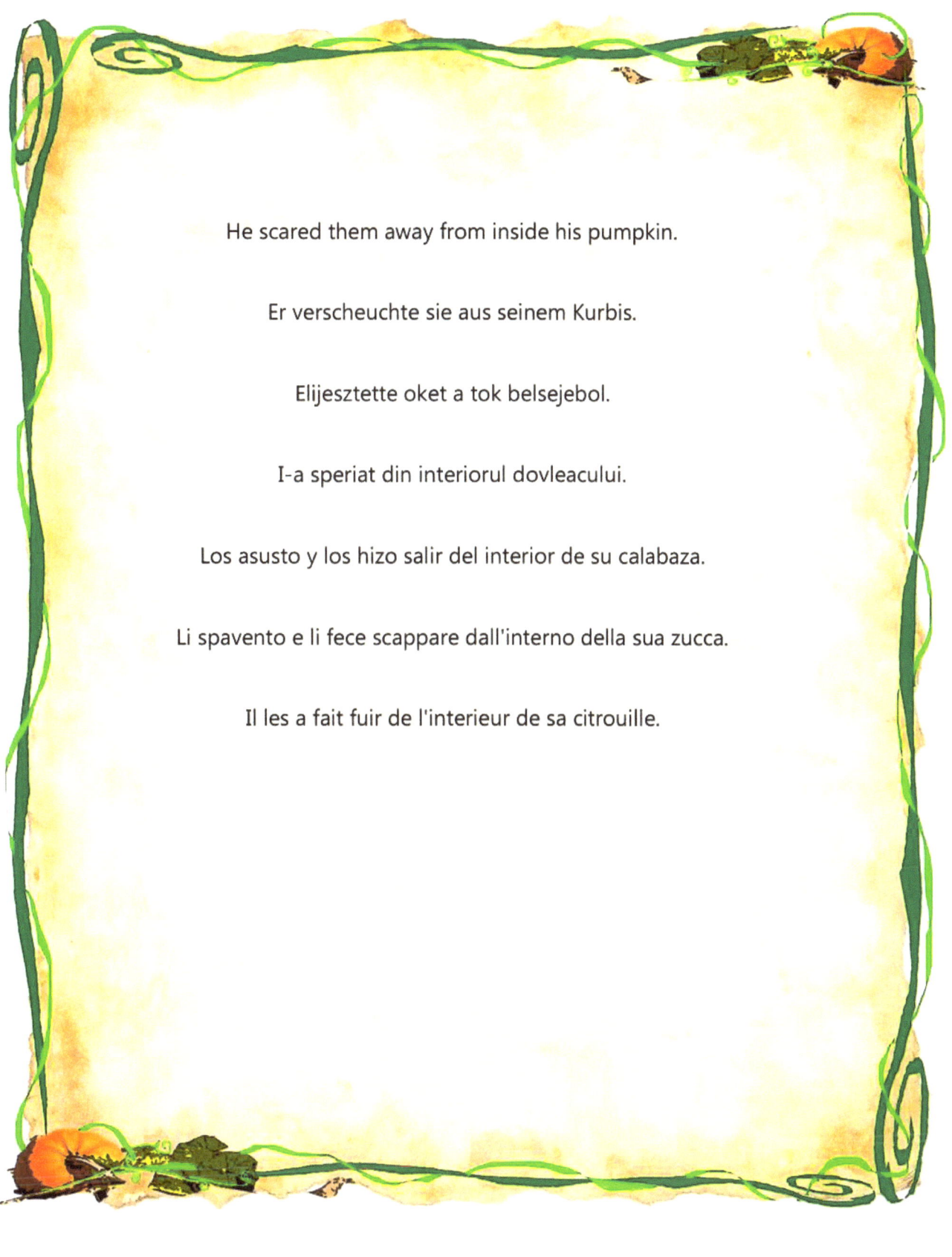

He scared them away from inside his pumpkin.

Er verscheuchte sie aus seinem Kurbis.

Elijesztette oket a tok belsejebol.

I-a speriat din interiorul dovleacului.

Los asusto y los hizo salir del interior de su calabaza.

Li spavento e li fece scappare dall'interno della sua zucca.

Il les a fait fuir de l'interieur de sa citrouille.

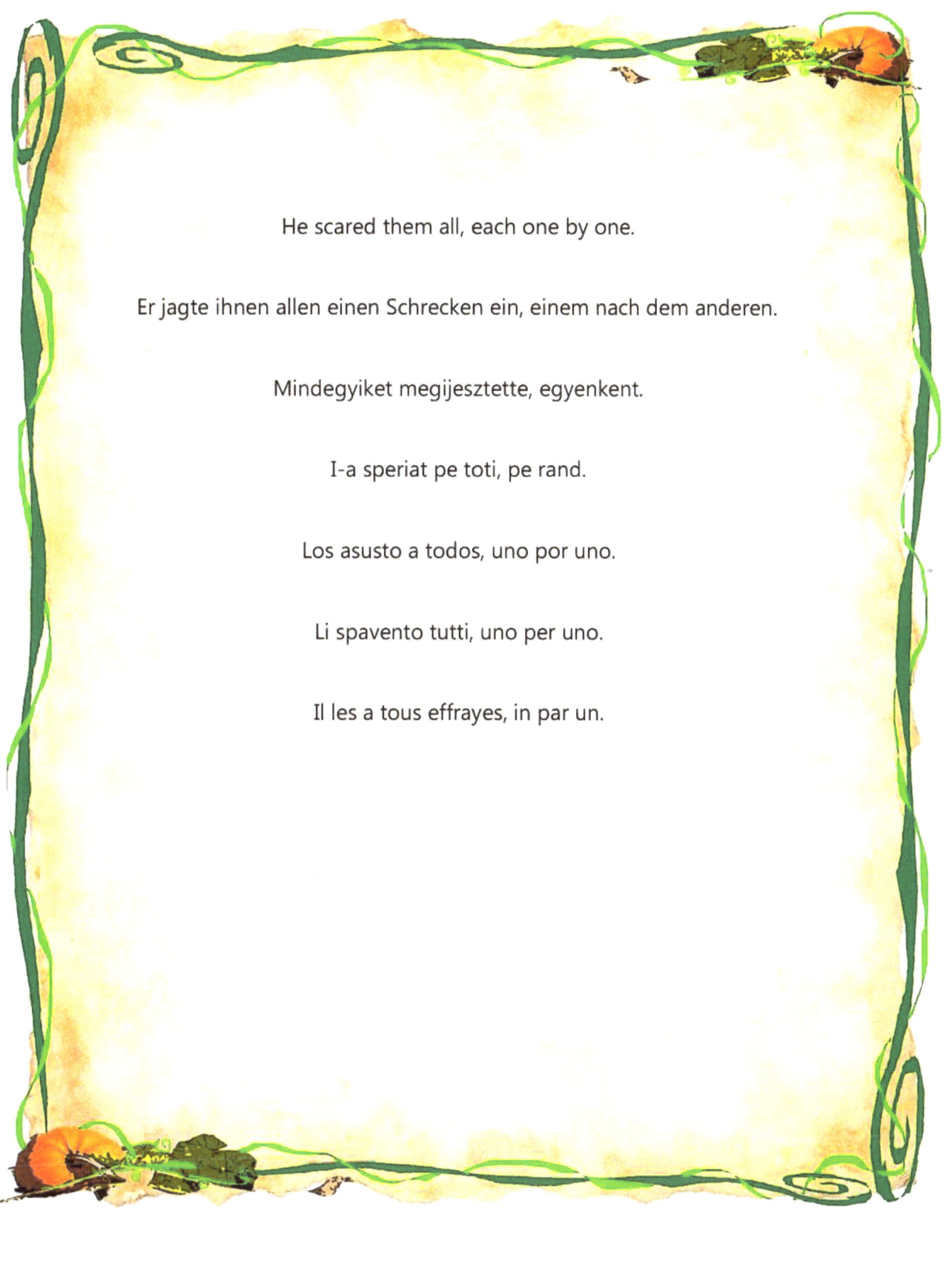

He scared them all, each one by one.

Er jagte ihnen allen einen Schrecken ein, einem nach dem anderen.

Mindegyiket megijesztette, egyenkent.

I-a speriat pe toti, pe rand.

Los asusto a todos, uno por uno.

Li spavento tutti, uno per uno.

Il les a tous effrayes, in par un.

He scared them away, away they would run!

Er verscheuchte sie und sie rannten weg.

Eliasztotta oket, elfutottak.

I-a speriat, au fugit.

El los asuto y ellos huyeron.

Li spavento e loro scapparono via.

Il les a fait fuir, et ils se sont enfuis.

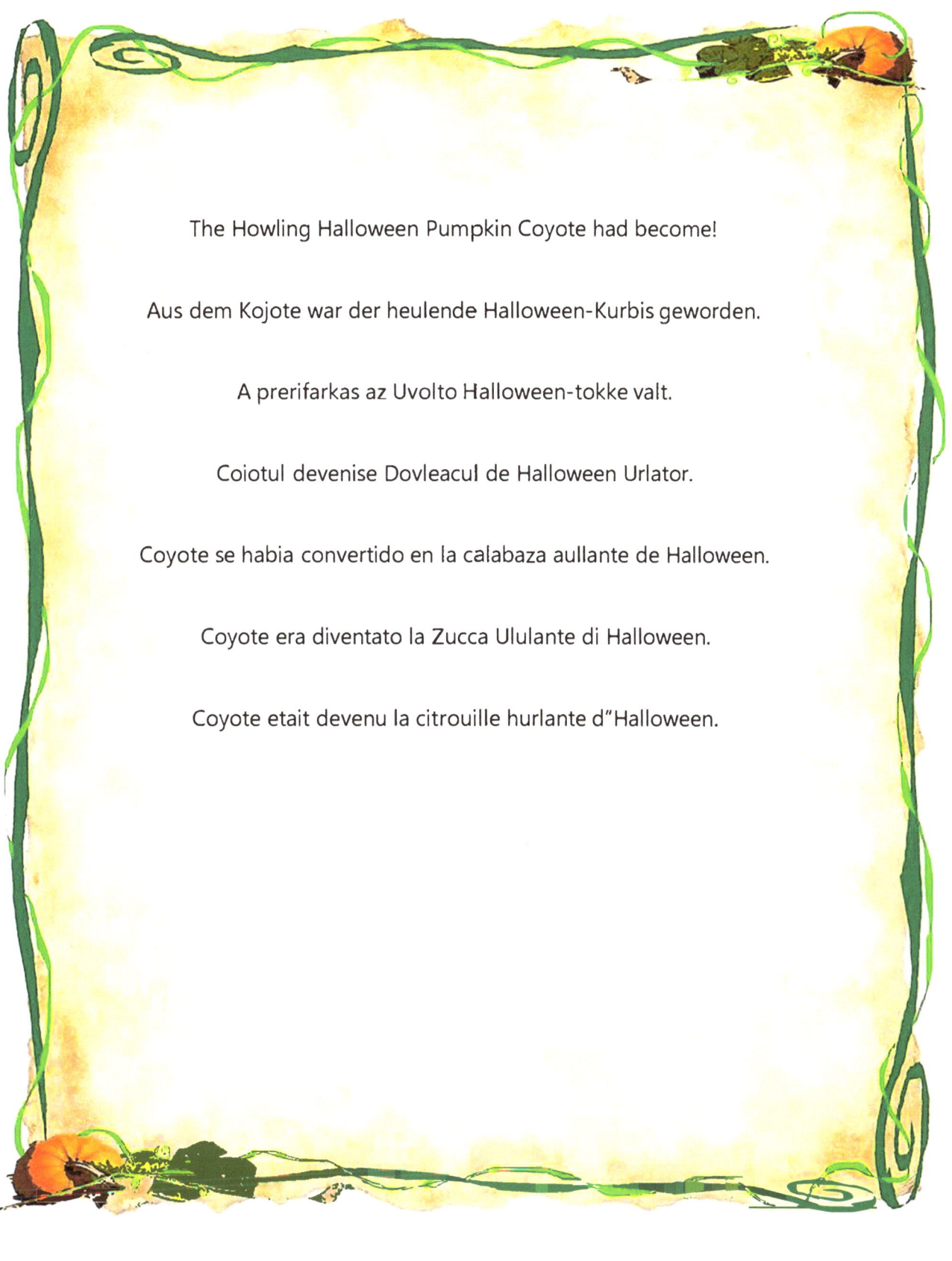

The Howling Halloween Pumpkin Coyote had become!

Aus dem Kojote war der heulende Halloween-Kurbis geworden.

A prerifarkas az Uvolto Halloween-tokke valt.

Coiotul devenise Dovleacul de Halloween Urlator.

Coyote se habia convertido en la calabaza aullante de Halloween.

Coyote era diventato la Zucca Ululante di Halloween.

Coyote etait devenu la citrouille hurlante d"Halloween.

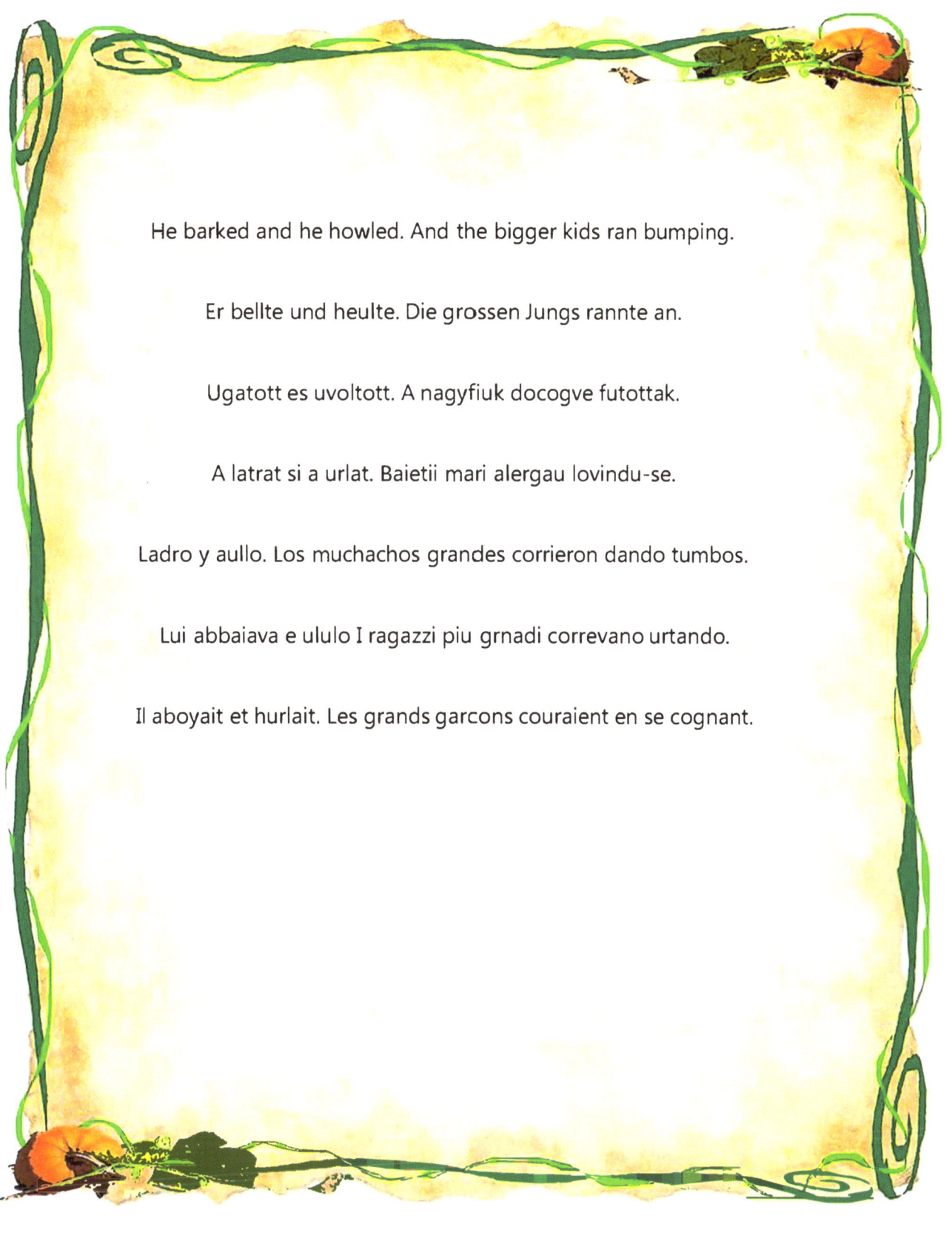

He barked and he howled. And the bigger kids ran bumping.

Er bellte und heulte. Die grossen Jungs rannte an.

Ugatott es uvoltott. A nagyfiuk docogve futottak.

A latrat si a urlat. Baietii mari alergau lovindu-se.

Ladro y aullo. Los muchachos grandes corrieron dando tumbos.

Lui abbaiava e ululo I ragazzi piu grnadi correvano urtando.

Il aboyait et hurlait. Les grands garcons couraient en se cognant.

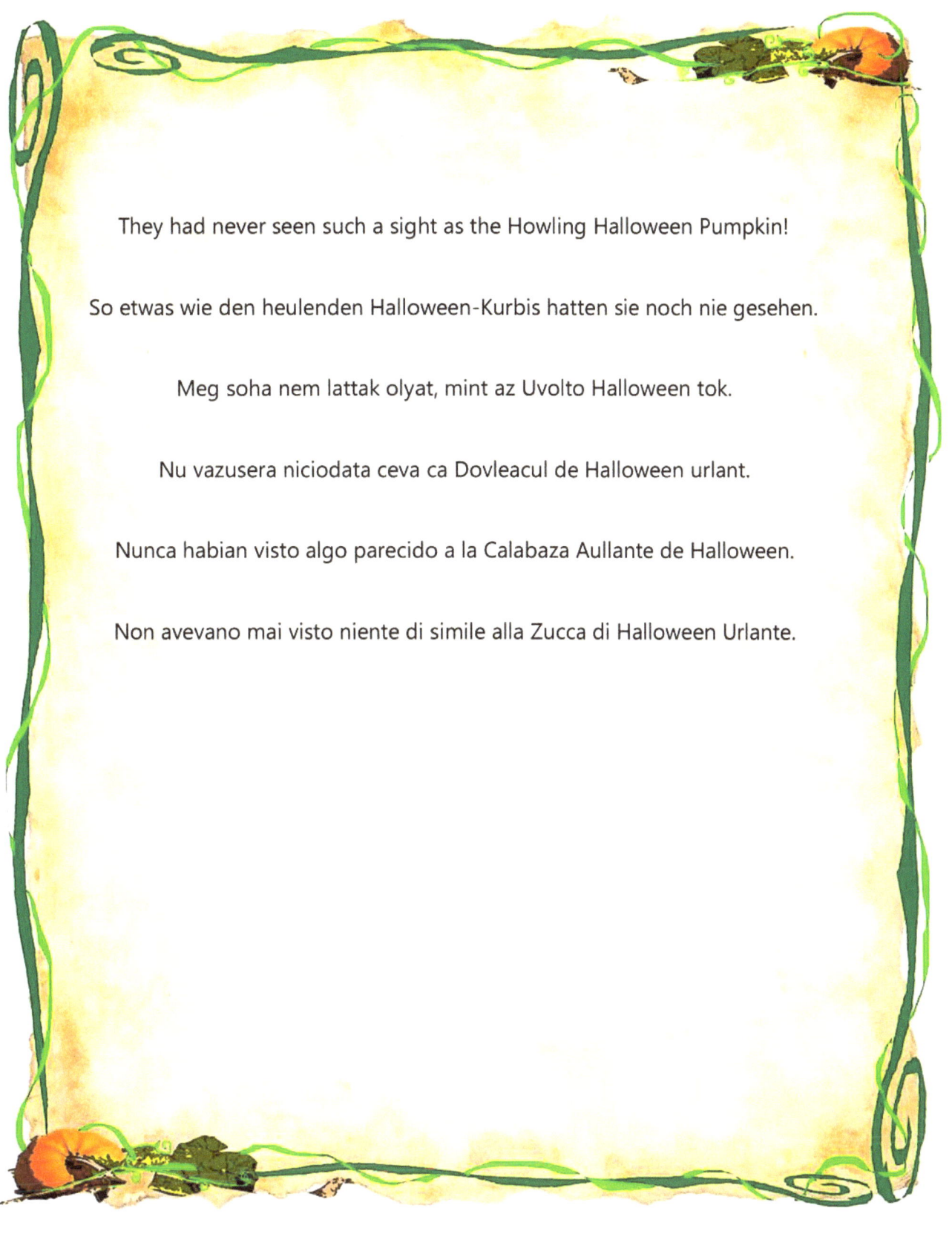

They had never seen such a sight as the Howling Halloween Pumpkin!

So etwas wie den heulenden Halloween-Kurbis hatten sie noch nie gesehen.

Meg soha nem lattak olyat, mint az Uvolto Halloween tok.

Nu vazusera niciodata ceva ca Dovleacul de Halloween urlant.

Nunca habian visto algo parecido a la Calabaza Aullante de Halloween.

Non avevano mai visto niente di simile alla Zucca di Halloween Urlante.

N. M. Reed and McCarthy Preston are the dynamic authors
of dozens of titles. They live in Northern California on a ranch with lots of animals and books.

"Adventures of Elf and Troll" series 1-6
"The Adventures of Elf and Troll: The Tattered Unicorn" series 7-12
"The Oak Grove of Maeve"
"Worrisome War of the Whimsical Wizards" or "The Dueling Wizards of Simpletown"
"Worrisome War of the Whimsical Wizards2: Dungeon For Dollars"
Home is Where the Horse Is : A Safer Place a true story of fire survival
The Glass Planet science fiction series
"The Littlest Coyote" and its coloring book and 9 languages
The Littlest Coyote Christmas and its coloring book
The Littlest Coyote and the Spotted Unicorn and coloring book
The Littlest Coyote Gets Spring Fever
The Littlest Coyote and Flowers the Donkey
The Littlest Coyote and the Howling Halloween Pumpkin
The Littlest Coyote Falls in Love
The Tattered Unicorn now in 4 languages
Bartimon the Boy Wizard and the Golden Squirrel

Available on Amazon.com
Walmart.com
Walmart and BarnesandNoble.com
and NMReedBooks.com
TatteredUnicronPublishing.com

Thank you for reading our stories!!
For more, visit:
TatteredUnicornPublishing.com